T0201544

Korean
Folktales

Korean Folktales

Classic Stories from Korea's Enchanted Past

RETOLD BY
KIM SO-UN & FRANCES CARPENTER

TUTTLE Publishing

Tokyo | Rutland, Vermont | Singapore

Contents

Korean
Folktales

The Man Who
Planted Onions

THIS STORY happened in an age before man ever ate onions. In those days people used to eat people. That was because everybody saw everybody else as cows, not as people at all. If you weren't careful, you'd mistake your own father and mother or your brothers and sisters for cows and eat them up. Surely there can be no sadder plight than this—for people not to be able to tell the difference between people and cows.

Once there was a man who made just such a mistake. He ate up his own brother! After a while he realized what he had done, but by then it was too late. There was nothing he could do to make amends.

"Oh, this is terrible, terrible!" he cried. "I hate living in this place!"

The man then left his home and started on a long journey in search of a place where people saw people as people and not as cows.

"Surely, in this wide, wide world there must be a country when men are men and cows are cows. I don't care how long it takes—I must find such a country."

And so he wandered over the world. He traveled deep into the mountains. He journeyed over the sea. No matter where he went, he still found that people ate each other. However, the man refused to give up hope and continued his quest.

He saw many an autumn and many a winter.

The man was young when he started out on his travels. Now he was no longer young. He was an old man. He continued his search, growing older and older. At long last, he came to a country which he had never seen nor heard of before.

Although he didn't yet realize it, this was the country he had been looking for all these long, long years. The inhabitants were all living happily together. Cows were cows, and people were people. They were clearly distinguished.

The aged traveler met up with an old man of this country, who greeted him: "Hello! Where are you from? And where are you going?"

"I have no definite place in mind," answered the traveler. "I am only searching for a country where people do not eat each other. Do you think there is such a place in this wide world? I have been searching for such a country for many, many years."

"Oh my, you must have had a hard time," said the aged inhabitant. "We used to be like that here too. People used to look like cows to each other and very often brothers ate brothers and sons ate their parents. But that was all before we began eating onions."

"Onions?" The old traveler was greatly surprised. "What is that again? Onions? What are onions?"

"Come over here and see for yourself. Those green shoots growing out of the ground there are what we call onions."

The old inhabitant kindly led the aged traveler to a field of onions to show him the sprouting shoots. Not only did the inhabitant show the traveller what onions were, but he also taught the aged visitor in detail how onions were grown and how they were prepared for eating.

The old traveler was greatly pleased. He was given some onion seeds, and then he started on his return trip home.

"By just eating some onions, a person will be able to see his neighbors as human beings and not as cows," he kept telling himself over and over again. He wanted to get home as soon as he could to tell all his own people about his marvelous discovery. The journey home did not seem too long nor difficult.

At long last he reached his homeland. The first thing he did was to plow his garden and plant the precious onion seeds that had been given him. As soon as he finished planting the seeds, he was so happy that he hurried off to visit his old friends, whom he had not seen for many years.

But, no matter whom he met, he was mistaken for a cow. The people gathered about him and tried to catch him.

"No! No! Wrong. Look at me well. I am your friend. Don't you remember me?" he cried in a loud voice.

But his friends would not listen to him. "My, what a noisy

cow!" they said. "This one really is a cow, isn't he? Let's hurry and catch him."

At last, the old traveler was caught and eaten up by his friends that very day.

Soon after this incident, the people began to notice some strange green shoots, growing in a corner of the old man's vegetable garden. Someone plucked one of the green shoots and tasted it. It had a strange, but pleasing, smell.

This was the onion that the old traveler had planted. Of course, no one knew what it was. Nonetheless, all the people flocked to the garden to eat the strange shoots that had a queer but pleasant taste.

To everybody's surprise, after eating the green shoots, people no longer saw each other as cows. They saw each other as they were. No longer was it possible for people to mistake each other for cows.

The people suddenly realized what the old traveler had done. But it was too late to thank him for his efforts. They had already eaten him up. Yet, to this very day, the old man's kindness lives on in the gratitude of the people whom he made happy with the onions he planted.

Mountains and Rivers

MANY, many years ago there lived in the country of Heaven a king and his beautiful daughter. One day this lovely princess lost her favorite ring. It was a beautiful ring, which she loved dearly. Her father, the king, ordered all his people to look for the ring throughout the country. But it was not to be found anywhere.

Meanwhile, the princess wept and wailed over her loss. The king could not bear to see his daughter so unhappy. To quiet her sobbing, he told her: "We have searched everywhere in the country of Heaven, but the ring cannot be found. It must have dropped to earth. I will send one of my men to search for it there and to hurry and bring it back to you."

So the king ordered one of his retainers to go down to earth, and there to search for the ring the princess had lost.

You must remember that this happened a long, long time ago, when the earth was still young. It was one great stretch of mud. The retainer did not know where to start his search for the ring.

But he had to start somewhere. So he began digging into the mud with his hands. He dug here and there, scooping up the dirt into mounds. He ran his fingers over the ground, leaving deep marks in the surface of the earth.

It was not an easy task to find a small ring in all this mass of mud. But, at long last, he found the precious ring.

The princess was overjoyed and once again became her old happy self.

The deep holes which the retainer dug became oceans. The mounds of dirt he left behind became mountains. And the places where he ran his fingers through the earth became rivers.

That is why the earth now has mountains, rivers and seas.

A Dog Named Fireball

ONCE there was, in the world above the skies, a land called the Land of Darkness. It was one country of many in that world, just as we have a number of different nations in the human world.

This Land of Darkness, as its name implies, had no light whatever. It was a country of perpetual night. Day in day out, year in year out, darkness reigned over the land.

The people of this country were quite used to living without lights. By listening to differences in sounds and by feeling their way about, they were able to find what they wanted. The people were, indeed, expert at groping about in the dark. However, to tell the truth, everybody was deeply unhappy. They were all sick and tired of the evering blackness.

Their one cry was: "I wish we had some light! How wonderful it would be to have some light! I wish we could have both day and night, and not just night."

Of course, the king of the Land of Darkness also wanted light. "The human world below has its sun and its moon. Isn't there, I wonder, a way of getting some light?" This was the thought which continually ran through the king's mind.

Now, in the Land of Darkness there was a great number of dogs. Everybody had dogs and among them was one extraordinary animal. He was a great, shaggy creature, but enormously strong and very clever.

This brave animal was endowed by nature with a gigantic mouth. Not only was his mouth exceptionally large, but it had the peculiar quality of being able to stand any kind of heat. The dog could carry hot things in his mouth—even red-hot balls of fire. Of course, in the Land of Darkness there were almost never any balls of fire, but even if there'd been a dozen a day, the dog could have carried them all. That is why the people of the Land of Darkness called him Fireball.

That was not all. He had four of the strongest and fastest legs in all the country. His legs were like steel pillars. He could run hundreds and thousands of miles in the twinkling of an eye.

One day the king had an idea. "Yes, that dog could surely run to the world of man, snatch away the sun, and bring it back to the Land of Darkness," the king thought.

The king called all the wise men of his kingdom together and told them of his idea. They listened to the king, and, when he had finished, one and all clapped their hands in approval and praised the wisdom of their ruler.

"That's it!" they said. "That's the only way to bring light to our country. Fireball will certainly succeed. You have really hit upon a wonderful idea."

Everyone was so overjoyed at the king's suggestion that they were completely carried away. They rejoiced as if Fireball had already brought the sun back in his mouth.

The king was happy too that he had thought of such a good plan. He ordered that preparations be made at once for Fireball's departure.

Fireball started out bravely on his long, long journey. Even with his fast legs, it would take Fireball two years to reach the sun. But the dog did not stop to rest. He kept on running and running, day after day, month after month. And at last he reached the skies over the earth.

There the bright sun was, shining in the sky. Soon he was right upon it. It was a huge, round ball of fire.

Fireball opened his enormous mouth and sank his teeth deeply into the sun, trying to tear it out of the sky. But it was hot—terribly hot. It was hotter than any fireball he had ever carried in his mouth before.

Fireball succeeded in getting the sun in his mouth, but he could not bear the heat. He felt as if his whole body would melt from the heat of the sun.

"It's no use. The sun is too hot. At this rate, I won't ever be able to tear the sun out of the sky," the dog said to himself. So he gave up and spit the sun out of his mouth. Then, filled with shame, he returned to the Land of Darkness.

When the king saw Fireball come back without the sun, he was very, very disappointed. Then he thought, "If the sun is too hot, then why not have him bring back the moon?"

"Go to the moon and bring it back," he commanded Fireball. "It should not be as hot as the sun." And so, even before Fireball was able to rest from his long trip to the sun, he was ordered to go to the moon.

After a long journey, Fireball again reached the skies over the human world. There the moon was, hanging from the sky. It shone with a blue-white light. Sure enough, it did not give off any heat.

"This time I shall be able to take back some light," thought Fireball.

He put his big mouth to the moon and took one bite, just as he had done with the sun. But, oh, it was so very, very cold! It was freezing cold, just like a big lump of ice. Fireball did succeed in getting all the moon into his mouth. But he could not bear

the cold. It seemed as if his whole body would freeze. So, once more, he had to give up. He spit the moon out and returned despondently to the Land of Darkness.

When the king saw Fireball come back without the moon, he was again very disappointed. But his wish to have light for his country remained unchanged. In fact, the more he thought of the sun and the moon and how difficult it was to get either, the more he wanted to have one or the other of them brought back. Again he called Fireball and ordered him to go get the sun.

Tired as he was, Fireball again set off bravely. But once again he failed. He did succeed in getting the sun into his mouth, but again he could not bear the heat. So once more Fireball came back to the Land of Darkness, empty-mouthed.

The king, sorely disappointed, next ordered Fireball to try for the moon again. But it was the same story. When he got the moon into his mouth, it was as cold as ever. He could not stand it. That was how cold the moon was.

Five times, ten times, twenty times, Fireball repeated the same journey. Each time the dog failed, the king's desire to bring light to his land became that much stronger.

But the sun was too hot, and the moon was too cold. No matter how brave and how strong Fireball was, this was one feat that he could not accomplish.

Still the king of the Land of Darkness would not give up. His desire to get light for his kingdom had now become a deeply fixed passion in his mind. He was sure that, no matter if Fireball failed a hundred times, a thousand times, there would come a day when the dog would finally succeed.

"Just watch," the king told himself. "One of these days Fireball will come home with either the sun or the moon."

So Fireball kept going to the sun and moon by turns. Many, many years passed. Fireball was no longer a young dog. He was no longer as strong and fleet as he once was. But the king of the Land of Darkness kept ordering the dog to go for the sun and the moon.

Even to this day Fireball continues his distant trips to the skies above the human world, first to the sun and then to the moon.

The eclipses of the sun and the moon are signs that Fireball, that brave and loyal dog from the Land of Darkness, is still living, still trying. Each time he grabs the sun or the moon in his mouth he is making another attempt to take light back to his king.

And, doubt it not, Fireball will go right on trying, again and again, until eternity. That's the kind of dog he is.

The Deer, the Rabbit, and the Toad

ONCE upon a time, a deer, a rabbit, and a toad lived together in one house. One day they held a great feast to celebrate a happy occasion.

The three began arguing over who should be served first. Finally it was decided that the oldest of the three should begin the feast. This started each of the three boasting of his age.

The deer spoke first. "When heaven and earth were first made," he said, "I helped put the stars in the sky. That shows how old I am. I surely must be the oldest here."

The rabbit then spoke up. "I planted the tree that was used to make the ladder for putting the stars in the sky. You see, I am older than Mr. Deer. So I must be the oldest here."

All this while the toad had sat silent, listening to the boasting of the others. All at once he began to sob quietly.

The deer and the rabbit were surprised and asked: "What's the matter, Mr. Toad?"

With tears running down his cheeks, the toad answered: "Your talk reminded me of my three sons. When they were still young they each planted a tree.

"When the trees grew up, my eldest son cut his down and from it made the handle for the hammer used in nailing the stars to the sky. From his tree my second son made the handle of the spade that was used to dig the channel where the Milky Way now flows. My youngest son used his tree to make the handle of the hammer which nailed the sun and the moon to the sky.

"But now, to my great sorrow, all three sons are dead and gone. I couldn't help but cry as I listened to you two arguing about your age."

At this, both the deer and the rabbit had to agree that Mr. Toad was surely the oldest of them all. So it was toad who was given the honor of being served first.

Mr. Bedbug's Feast

FATHER Bedbug was about to greet his sixty-first birthday. Now, in the country where Mr. Bedbug lived, it was the custom to celebrate one's sixty-first birthday in a grand manner, since few people lived that long, to say nothing of bedbugs.

Thus, Mr. Bedbug decided to hold a great feast and invited his two close friends, Mr. Flea and Mr. Louse.

Mr. Flea and Mr. Louse were both happy to be invited. They were sure there would be a groaning board, and both were delighted with the prospect of good food and much wine. They started out together in a very happy mood.

But Mr. Flea, like all of his kind, was a very short-tempered fellow by nature and, as he walked along with Mr. Louse, he became very impatient, for, as you know, Mr. Louse was a very slow walker. Mr. Flea couldn't help taking a few jumps ahead, and then a few more.

Left way behind, Mr. Louse called out: "Say, don't be so impatient! Slow down and wait for me!"

Mr. Flea felt ashamed and, for a time, held himself back to walk along side by side with Mr. Louse. But Mr. Louse was really slow. Sometimes it was even difficult to tell whether he was walking or standing still. You see, Mr. Louse took his time and was in no great hurry.

Seeing Mr. Louse so composed and quiet, Mr. Flea could not hold his patience any longer and said: "Mr. Louse, you come along afterwards. It irks me to walk so slowly." No sooner had Mr. Flea said this than he jumped ahead and was at Mr. Bedbug's home in no time.

Mr. Bedbug had really prepared a grand feast for his friends. There were many, many dishes and much wine, all laid out on a large table.

Panting from his hurried walk, Mr. Flea called out to Mr. Bedbug, even before he entered the house, saying: "Oh, but I'm thirsty! Please give me some wine."

"Why, yes," said Mr. Bedbug, "do have some of the wine. But why, in heaven's name, did you rush here on such a warm day?" He filled a large bowl to the brim with wine and gave it to Mr. Flea.

Mr. Flea gulped the wine down greedily. Then he said: "Ah, at last I feel refreshed. But I would like another bowl, I think."

And so he drank another bowlful of wine.

Mr. Bedbug and Mr. Flea waited for Mr. Louse to arrive. They waited and waited, but there was no sign of him.

At last, Mr. Bedbug stood up and said: "It's quite a distance for Mr. Louse to walk. Maybe I should go out to meet him."

After Mr. Bedbug was gone, Mr. Flea was left all alone. The sight of all that food on the table and all that wine in the bottle began to torment him. He was already slightly drunk from his two bowlfuls of wine, and he simply couldn't resist the temptation. Slowly he reached for the wine bottle and filled his bowl.

He drank one bowlful—two bowlfuls—three bowlfuls. Finally he lost count—and suddenly there was not a single drop of wine left in the bottle.

Soon Mr. Bedbug returned with his other guest, Mr. Louse. They found Mr. Flea lying on the floor, dead drunk, snoring away noisily. They also noticed that there was no more wine left.

Poor Mr. Louse—he had come all this distance to the party, and now there was not so much as a drop of wine left for him. Losing his usual composure, he became very angry.

Suddenly he began kicking Mr. Flea in the back, crying: "Wake up, you impudent thing!"

Mr. Flea woke up with a start. But he was still so drunk that he didn't know what was what, nor why. He couldn't even remember what he had done.

"What's the big idea of kicking me in the back?" he shouted angrily at Mr. Louse.

This, of course, was enough to start a big fight between Mr. Flea and Mr. Louse. Each fought in anger, and neither one would give in to the other. The party was quite ruined.

Mr. Bedbug tried to stop them. He tried to push the two apart, crying: "Here, here! Stop this foolish fighting!"

But Mr. Flea and Mr. Louse were locked tightly together. Suddenly they both toppled over, with a great crash. And where should they fall but right on the very top of Mr. Bedbug's stomach!

Poor Mr. Bedbug—his stomach has never mended from that fall. It is still flat to this day.

Mr. Louse—he bruised his hip when he fell. And even today, he still has a black bruise on his hip.

And what of Mr. Flea? Even today his face has the red flush it got from all that wine he drank.

Why We Have Earthquakes

THIS story goes back to the beginning of time. One corner of the floor of Heaven began to sag. It seemed as if Heaven itself would topple over and crash. The king of Heaven became greatly alarmed and ordered a huge pillar of red copper to be made.

What he wanted to do was to use this big pillar to bolster up the sagging corner of Heaven. So he ordered that the pillar be built on the surface of the Earth below. But the ground was so soft and Heaven so heavy that the whole pillar kept sinking into the dirt and was useless in holding up the sagging corner of Heaven.

The king of Heaven then searched throughout all his land for the strongest man in his kingdom. Finally he found a man who was enormously strong. He sent this man to Earth and told him to hold the huge copper pillar up on his shoulder. Only in this way was the corner of Heaven finally strengthened and the sagging corrected.

And so, as long as the strong man held the pillar up, Heaven was safe. But he could never take his shoulder away, lest Heaven come crashing down.

So, even to this day, the strong man supports the copper pillar. But, of course, the pillar and Heaven are heavy, and the weight becomes painful on his shoulder. So every once in a while, the strong man must shift the weight from one shoulder to the other. Every time this happens, the ground quivers and quakes with the man's effort. That is why we have earthquakes.

The Stupid Noblewoman

ONCE there was a nobleman's wife who was rather stupid.

One day, the father of her daughter's husband passed away, and the noblewoman went to express her sympathies to the bereaved family. When she arrived at the house, she found the whole family and all the relatives gathered together.

"*Ai-go, ai-go!*" they were all crying in sorrow, for, you see, in Korea there is no cry of greater sorrow than this.

When the noblewoman saw this weeping, she felt that she too must express sorrow in the same way. So she joined in the wailing too, sobbing, "*Ai-go, ai-go, ai-go!*" with the best of them.

As she cried she forgot who it was that had passed away. She was so moved by her own tears that soon she was thinking it was her own husband who had died. "O my husband, my dear, dear husband!" she wailed. "Take me with you!"

The people around her were astonished at first, but soon they burst out in great laughter.

The foolish noblewoman could not understand why the people were laughing, and she continued weeping. Between sobs she said: "My husband, my dear, dear husband, why have you left me? Please take me with you!"

She had repeated this several times when her daughter quietly poked her in the ribs. The noblewoman suddenly realized that she was not at home but was attending the funeral of her daughter's father-in-law. She saw she had made a big mistake and wondered how she could make amends.

Suddenly she turned around and faced the people gathered there and greeted them politely. Hoping to made them feel better after what she had done, she said: "You are all well, I hope. Is there no great change in the family?"

The people looked at her in surprise. "You ask if there is any change. Could there be a greater change than to have the master of the house pass away?" they asked in utter astonishment.

"Oh, yes," the stupid noblewoman answered, "of course. And what sickness did the master die of?"

"A hammer fell off the shelf—" they began.

But, even before they could finish the sentence, the noblewoman, all eager to be polite, exclaimed: "My, how dangerous! And did he hurt himself? Was it a bad accident?"

"Of course he hurt himself. The master died from the injury caused by the falling hammer. What greater accident could there be?"

When she heard this, the stupid noblewoman became very embarrassed. She realized that everything she had said had only made her seem the more foolish. She racked her brains for something to say that would make things right again. Her gaze wandered to the window, and outside she saw a magpie perched on a bough of a persimmon tree.

Smiling her best smile, the noblewoman pointed to the bird and said: "My, how beautiful! Is that your magpie?"

All the people gathered in the house sat for a moment in stunned silence. Then suddenly they broke into uncontrollable gales of laughter, while the noblewoman sat looking more stupid than ever.

The Tiger and the Rabbit

ONCE a hungry old tiger was walking through the woods, looking for something to eat. By chance he came upon a baby rabbit. The old tiger's eyes glistened to see such a juicy morsel.

"I'm going to eat you up," he told the rabbit.

The baby rabbit, though very small, was a clever fellow. He coolly answered: "Just wait, Mr. Tiger. I'm still too young and small to make good eating. I have something much tastier for you. I shall give you some rice cakes. When you toast them over a fire, they are really delicious."

As he said this, the rabbit stealthily picked up eleven small white stones. He showed them to the tiger.

The greedy tiger became very interested. "But," he said, "how do you eat these?"

The rabbit answered: "Here, I'll show you. You toast them over a fire until they are red-hot, and then you eat them in one gulp. I'll go find some firewood so you can have some right away."

The rabbit gathered together some twigs and sticks and started a fire. The tiger put the eleven stones on the fire and watched them toast.

When the stones were getting hot and red, the rabbit said: "Mr. Tiger, wait a while. If you put soy sauce on the cakes, they will taste even more delicious. I'll get some for you. So hold on for a moment and don't eat any while I am gone. . . . Let's see, there are ten rice cakes, aren't there?" So saying, the baby rabbit skipped into the woods and ran toward the village.

As the stones reddened with the heat, the tiger began licking his lips in anticipation. He started counting what he thought were rice cakes.

"One, two, three... Why," he said in surprise, "there are eleven cakes, not ten."

He started counting them over again, but, no matter how many times he counted, there was always one too many.

"The baby rabbit said there were ten. If I ate one, he wouldn't know the difference," the tiger said to himself.

So he quickly took the reddest one from the fire, popped it in his mouth, and gulped it down greedily. But, oh, it was hot! so very, very hot! The tiger not only burnt his mouth and tongue, but his stomach as well. He squirmed with pain. He moaned and groaned and rolled all over the ground.

All of which served the old tiger right for being so greedy. It was some time before he could eat anything again.

One day, much later, the tiger met the baby rabbit again.

"Say you, you bad rabbit! What a time you gave me the other day. I'll not let you go *this* time. Now I'll really eat you up." And the tiger's eyes burned with anger.

But the baby rabbit did not look a bit frightened. With a smile he answered: "Don't be so angry, Mr. Tiger. Please listen to me. I have found a way to catch hundreds and thousands of sparrows. All you have to do is to keep perfectly still with your mouth wide open. The sparrows will come flying right into your mouth and make a nice feast for you."

The old tiger licked his lips and asked: "Oh, is that so? What else am I supposed to do?"

"Oh, it isn't difficult at all. All you need do is to look up at the sky and keep your mouth open. I'll chase the sparrows out of the bamboo thicket into your mouth."

Once again the old tiger did as he was told.

The baby rabbit hopped into the bamboo thicket and set fire to a pile of dry leaves and twigs. The sound made by the burning leaves and twigs was just like the fluttering of thousands of sparrows.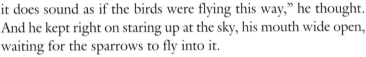

The tiger, meanwhile, kept gazing up at the sky, his mouth wide open. "Why, it does sound as if the birds were flying this way," he thought. And he kept right on staring up at the sky, his mouth wide open, waiting for the sparrows to fly into it.

From a distance, the baby rabbit cried: "Shoo! shoo!" pretending he was chasing sparrows.

"Mr. Tiger, Mr. Tiger, a lot of birds are flying your way now. Don't move! Just wait a while longer."

So saying, the baby rabbit scampered away to safety.

The fire came closer and closer to the tiger, and the noise became louder and louder. The tiger was sure the birds were coming his way, and he patiently waited. Soon the sound was all around him, but not a single sparrow popped into his mouth.

"That's funny," thought the tiger, and he took his eyes from the sky and looked around him. To his surprise, there was one great ocean of fire all about him as far as he could see.

The tiger became frantic with fear as he fought his way through the burning woods. Finally he managed to come through alive, but his fur was all sizzled black. And his skin looked like newly tanned hide.

It was soon winter. Once again the tiger became ravenous. As he stalked through the forest looking for food, he came to the banks of a river. There he saw his old friend, the baby rabbit, eating some vegetables.

The tiger roared angrily at the rabbit: "How dare you fool me about the sparrows! I won't let you get away with anything *this* time. I will eat you up for sure." He ground his teeth and ran up to the rabbit.

The rabbit smiled as usual and said: "Hello, Mr. Tiger, it's quite some time since we last met, isn't it? Look, I was just fishing with my tail in the river. I caught a big one, and it was delicious. Don't you think river fish are very tasty?"

The hungry tiger gulped with hunger and said: "You were fishing with your tail? Show me how it is done."

"It isn't very easy," the rabbit replied, "but I'm sure you will be able to do it. All you need to do is to put your tail in the water and shut your eyes. I shall go up the river a little and chase the fish this way. Remember, you mustn't move. Just wait a little, and you'll have many fish biting at your tail."

The old tiger did what the rabbit told him. He put his tail into the river, closed his eyes, and waited.

The rabbit ran up the river bank and hopped about here and there, pretending to chase the fish down to where the tiger was waiting. The winter day was beginning to wane, and the water became colder and colder.

"The fish are beginning to swim your way, Mr. Tiger," the rabbit shouted. "They will be biting on your tail any minute. Don't move!" Then the rabbit ran away.

The river began to freeze over slowly. The old tiger moved his tail from side to side. It was heavy. "Ah, good! I must have caught a lot of fish on my tail. Just a while longer and I shall have a good catch," he told himself.

He waited until midnight. "Now I shall have lots of fish to eat," thought the tiger.

So he tried to pull his tail out. But it wouldn't move! What had happened? Why, his tail was frozen tightly in the ice.

"Oh, I've been tricked again," moaned the tiger. But it was too late to do anything.

When it became light, the villagers came to the river and found the old tiger trapped in the ice. Thus the greedy old tiger was finally caught and taken away. And that was one greedy old tiger who never ate another rabbit.

The Great Flood

ONCE upon a time, long, long ago, there lived a handsome boy named Talltree. He was so named because his father was a tree—a tree so tall that it almost reached the sky. His mother was a celestial being, a beautiful creature from Heaven who came down to earth from time to time. She often used to rest in the shade of the tall tree. In time she became the tree's wife and gave birth to a child: Talltree.

When he was about eight years old, his mother left him beside his father, the great, tall tree, and returned to her home in the heavens.

One day a terrible storm arose suddenly. For days on end the rains poured down on earth, until all the ground was under water. Soon mountainous waves began sweeping toward the tall tree, the father of the young boy.

Father-tree became alarmed. He called to his child and said: "I shall soon be uprooted by this terrible storm. When I fall, you must climb into my branches and perch on my back. Otherwise, you will be drowned."

The storm became more and more violent. Lashed by screaming winds, great waves thundered against the trunk of the tree. Then came the fiercest gust of all, and the kingly tree fell with a crash.

Quickly the boy climbed on his father's back and held tightly to the branches. The great tree floated on the rushing waters. For days and days it drifted on and on, at the mercy of the angry waves.

One day they came upon a great number of ants struggling in the water. The poor ants, on the point of drowning, cried: "Save us! Save us!"

Talltree felt sorry for them and asked his father: "Shall we save the ants?"

"Yes," his father replied.

"Climb up on my father's back," Talltree called to the ants, "and you will be saved. Hurry! Hurry!"

Talltree helped the tired and weary ants get up out of the wind-whipped water onto the tree. The ants, of course, were very happy to be saved.

Soon, a great cloud of mosquitoes came flying through the storm. They were also weary and couldn't find a place to land and rest their tired wings.

"Help! Help!" the mosquitoes buzzed.

Again, Talltree asked: "Father, shall we save the mosquitoes?"

"Yes," his father replied.

So Talltree helped the tired mosquitoes landed on the leaves and branches of his father's back. The mosquitoes were also very grateful to be saved from the cruel storm.

As Talltree and his father and the ants and the mosquitoes drifted along, they heard the cry of a child. They looked into the waves and saw it was a boy about the same age as Talltree.

"Save me! Save me!" cried the boy.

Talltree felt sorry for the boy. "Let's save the boy too," he said. But this time his father didn't answer.

Again the cries of the boy came pitifully across the raging waters. And again Talltree said: "Please, Father, let's save that boy."

Still there was no answer from Father-tree.

Talltree pleaded with him a third time: "Father, we must save that poor boy!"

The father finally answered: "Do as you wish. I leave it up to you."

Talltree was overjoyed and called to the boy to come and climb up onto his father's back. So the boy was saved too.

Eventually, Talltree, his father, the ants, the mosquitoes, and the boy who had been saved from the waves came to an island. It was the peak of the highest mountain in that country—a mountain as high as Paik Tu, the Mountain with a White Head, so called because the snows never melted from its crest.

As soon as the tree reached the island, the ants and the mosquitoes thanked Talltree and departed.

The two boys were very hungry, for they had not eaten for many days. They wandered over the island searching for food and finally came upon a small straw-thatched hut.

"Please give us some food," the boys cried out.

An old woman and two young girls came out. They welcomed the boys into the house and gave them food. One of the girls was the real daughter of the old woman and the other an adopted child.

The great flood and storm had destroyed everything on earth except this little island. The only people left in the world were the two boys, the old woman, and the two girls. There was no other place where the boys could stay. So from that day forth they lived with the old woman, working for her as servants.

It was a peaceful life. The days slipped into weeks, the weeks into months, and the months into years, and the boys grew into strong, fine youths.

As the old woman watched the boys grow into manhood, she thought to herself: "They will make fine husbands for my two girls."

One day, she called the two of them to her and said: "Whichever of you is the more skillful shall have my own daughter for his wife, and the other shall have my adopted girl."

Now the old woman's own daughter was the more beautiful of the two girls, and the boy who had been saved by Talltree during the flood wanted very much to marry her. He thought of a way to get her for his own wife.

"Grandma," he said, "Talltree has a strange power which none of the rest of us has. For example, you can mix a whole sack of millet in a pile of sand, and he can have the millet and the sand separated in no time. Let him try it and show you."

The old woman was astounded to hear this. "Is that so?" she said. "I would like very much to see his wonderful ability. Come, Talltree, let me see if you really can do this amazing thing."

Talltree knew he was being tricked. He knew he certainly could do no such thing. He knew the other youth was planning to get him into trouble. So he refused. But the old woman was adamant. She was determined that Talltree should show her his strange power.

"If you don't do it, or if you can't do it, I won't give you my daughter in marriage," the old woman said.

Talltree saw he couldn't resist and sighed. "Very well, then," he said, "I'll try."

The old woman emptied a sack of millet into a pile of sand and mixed them together. Then she left, saying she would return in a short while to see how he was getting along.

Talltree gazed hopelessly at the pile of millet and sand. What was he to do? It was not humanly possible to sort the millet from the sand.

Suddenly, Talltree felt something bite his heel. He looked down, and there he saw a large ant.

"What is troubling you, Talltree?" the ant asked. "I suppose you no longer remember me, but I am one of the ants you saved a long time ago in the flood. Tell me, what's the matter?"

Talltree told the ant how he must separate the millet from the sand or else not be able to marry the old woman's daughter.

"Is that all? Don't you worry, my friend. Just leave it to me."

No sooner had the ant said this than a great mass of ants came swarming from all over the place. They attacked the huge pile of sand and millet, each ant carrying a millet grain in its mouth

and putting it into the sack placed nearby. Back and forth the ants hurried. In no time, all of the millet was back in the sack.

When the old woman came back, she was amazed to find that Talltree had finished an impossible task in so short a time.

The other youth was surprised too, and chagrined that his trick had failed. But he still wished to marry the old woman's daughter and pleaded with her: "Please give me your real child for my wife."

The old woman hesitated. She thought for a moment and replied: "You are both very dear to me. I must be absolutely fair. Tonight will be a moonless night. I shall put my two daughters each in a separate room. One will be in the east room and the other in the west room. You two will stay outside and when I say 'ready,' you will both come into the house and go to the room of your choice. The girl you find there will be your bride. I'm sure this is the best and fairest plan."

That night the two youths waited outside for the old woman's command.

Suddenly Talltree heard a mosquito flying close to his ear.

"Buss, buzz," said the mosquito, in a wee voice. "Talltree, you must go to the east room. Buzz, buzz. Remember, it is the east room."

Talltree was overjoyed to hear this. He felt sure the mosquito was one he had saved during the flood. "Ready!" the old woman cried out.

The two boys went into the house. While the other boy was still hesitating, Talltree went straight to the east room. There he found the old woman's biological daughter. She became his wife.

The other youth could not complain. So he took the other girl for his wife.

Both couples were very, very happy. They had many, many children and lived happily ever after. In time, their children and their grandchildren and their great-grandchildren spread throughout the world. And again the earth was filled with people.

The Blind Mouse

ONCE there was a very selfish girl. This girl was completely spoiled. Never in her life had she ever said yes to anything. If something displeased her, even in the slightest, she would fuss and fume and fret and make her parents miserable. At the same time, she had to have her own way about everything. She would never listen to others and always wanted her own wishes granted right away.

No matter how often her mother and father told her how bad she was, it did not seem to have any effect. She was always the same spoiled girl.

"What will happen to this child of ours?" This was all her parents ever worried about.

One day this little girl was sitting all by herself in her room, when a small mouse came scampering out of its hole.

"My, how horrible!" she cried in surprise. But, because the mouse was so small and cute, she did not feel afraid. She sat perfectly still and waited to see what would happen.

The little mouse ran here and there around the room in search of something to eat. In one corner of the room a few grains of rice had been spilled. When the mouse found the rice, strangely enough, it didn't gobble it up, but instead scurried back into its hole.

In a little while, out it came again. This time it was not alone. Out followed a larger mouse. It was the mother mouse.

The little mouse led the mother mouse to the grains of rice. She sniffed around until she found them piled on the floor.

"Squeak, squeak," the mother mouse cried in delight. Then she hungrily gobbled up the rice grains.

You see, the mother mouse was blind. She could not find food for herself without help. So the little mouse always searched out food for the mother mouse.

Presently there was the sound of footsteps outside.

The little mouse cried: "Squeak, squeak, Mother! We must hurry home." Then, it led its mother back into their hole, guarding her all the while with care.

The spoiled girl had been watching this from beginning to end. Now she became thoroughly ashamed of herself. "Why even a little mouse loves and cares for its mother like that. What a bad girl I have been," she told herself.

After that, she changed so completely that everybody thought she was a different girl. Praised now for being a good child, she never told anyone about the little mouse and its blind mother.

The Pheasant's Bell

DEEP in a lonely forest there once lived a woodcutter. One day the woodcutter was at work felling trees, when he heard the cry of a pheasant and the fluttering of wings nearby. He wondered what was happening and went to see what the commotion was about. Under the shade of a bush he saw a pheasant nest with many eggs inside it. A great snake was poised to strike at a mother pheasant, who was bravely trying to defend her nest. The woodcutter picked up a stick and tried to scare the snake away, crying: "Go away! Go away!" But the snake wouldn't move, so the woodcutter struck it with his stick and killed it.

Some years after this, the woodcutter one day set out on a distant journey. Twilight found him walking along a lonely mountain path. Soon it became completely dark. He was hungry and tired. Suddenly, far ahead of him in the woods he saw a dim light. He walked toward the light and came to a large and beautiful straw-thatched house. The woodcutter was surprised, for he had never expected to find such a fine house so deep in the forest. He knocked on the door, and a beautiful young woman, about nineteen or twenty years of age, came out.

"I am hungry and tired," the woodcutter told her. "I have walked a long way today and have no place to stay. I wonder if you would put me up for the night?"

The girl answered in a kind tone: "I am alone in this house, but please do come in."

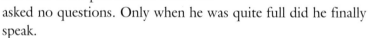

She welcomed the woodcutter inside and spread out a grand feast for him. But the woodcutter felt very ill at ease. He could not understand why this young woman should be living all alone in the middle of a forest. He couldn't help wondering if he hadn't entered a haunted house.

But he was so hungry that he ate the fine food put before him and asked no questions. Only when he was quite full did he finally speak.

"Why should such a young person as you live all alone here in such a large house?" he asked.

"I am waiting to take my revenge against my enemy," the woman answered.

"Your enemy?" he asked. "Where would he be?"

"He is right here," she said. "See, you are my enemy!" Then she opened a great red mouth and laughed loudly.

The woodcutter was astounded and asked her why he should be her enemy.

She reminded him of the time he had saved the mother pheasant and her nest, and added: "I am the snake you killed that time. I've waited a long long time to meet up with you. And now I'm going to take your life. Then finally I'll have the revenge I've dreamed of for so long."

When the woodcutter heard this, his heart sank. "I had nothing against you at that time," he said in a quavering voice. "It was simply because I couldn't bear to see helpless beings hurt by someone strong like you were. That's why I saved the pheasant. But I really didn't mean to kill you. Don't say I'm your enemy. Please, please spare my life."

At first the woman kept laughing at him and would not listen to his pleas. But he kept on pleading, falling to his bended knees, with tears flowing down his cheeks.

"All right then," the girl said, "I'll give you one chance. Deep in the forest and high in the mountains there is a temple ruin. Not a single soul lives there. However, a huge bell hangs in that temple. If, before dawn, you are able to ring that bell without moving from the place where you're sitting now, then I'll spare your life."

When the woodcutter heard this, he was even more frightened. "How can I ring that bell while I'm still sitting here in this room?" he sighed. "You're unfair. I'm no better off than before. Please don't say such a cruel thing. It's the same as killing me right now. Please let me go home."

The woman firmly refused: "No! You are the enemy I've waited for so long. Yes, I've waited a long time for this chance to avenge myself. Now that I have you in my hands, why should I let you go? If you can't ring the bell, resign your-self to death. I shall eat you up."

The woodcutter gave up all hope. He realized that he was as good as dead.

Suddenly, the quiet night air vibrated with the sound of a distant bell. "Bong!" the bell rang. Yes, it was the bell in the crumbling old mountain temple!

When the woman

heard the bell, she turned white and gnashed her teeth. "It's no use," she said. "You must be guarded by the gods."

No sooner had she said this than she disappeared from sight. The fine house in which the woodcutter was sitting also disappeared in a puff of smoke.

The woodcutter, whose life had been so miraculously saved, could hardly wait for daylight to break. With the first sign of dawn, he set off toward the mountains in search of the ruined temple, filled with gnawing curiosity.

Sure enough, as he had been told, there he found a temple in which hung a great bell. But there was not a single soul in sight. The woodcutter looked at the bell in wonder. On it he noticed a stain of blood. He looked down to the floor. There, with head shattered and wings broken, lay the bloodstained body of a pheasant.

The Grateful Tiger

ONCE upon a time a huge tiger lay groaning and moaning by the roadside. A young student happened to pass by and see the suffering animal. He drew near, half in fear, and asked: "What is the matter, tiger? Have you hurt yourself?"

The tiger, tears filling his eyes, opened its mouth as if to show the student that there was something wrong inside.

"Let me see," the student said, "maybe I can help." The student peered into the tiger's mouth and there saw a sharp bone splinter stuck in the animal's throat.

"Oh, you poor thing!" the student said. "There's a bone stuck in your throat. Here, let me take it out. Easy now, it will soon be better." The student stuck his hand into the tiger's mouth and gently pulled the bone out.

The tiger licked the student's hands and looked up into his face with tears of relief and gratitude, as if to say: "Thank you, thank you for your kindness." Then, bowing low many times, the tiger walked toward the woods, turning to look back from time and time at the student.

That night, as he slept, the student had a strange dream. A mysterious woman, whom he had never seen before, appeared in his sleep and said: "I am the tiger you saved today. Thanks to your gentle kindness, I was spared much pain and suffering. I shall surely show my gratitude to you some day." With that, she faded away.

Many years passed. The young student who had helped the tiger was now ready to take his final examinations in the capital city. As he rode along toward the capital he was thinking that if he passed these examinations he would become a government official and would one day become rich and famous. But many, many students came to take the tests from all over the country. In fact, there were so many applicants, the competition made it difficult to be chosen for the job.

The student prayed in his heart that he would be among the fortunate ones chosen for the coveted position. But it was not to be. There were just too many people ahead of him.

The youth was very despondent. "I have come such a long,

long way to the city. But I suppose it can't be helped; I'll return home, study hard, and try again next year." In this way he resigned himself to his failure and prepared to return to his home in the country the next day.

That night, however, the young student again had a dream. Again the strange woman appeared and said: "Don't be discouraged. Keep your chin up. It's still too early to despair. I shall repay you for the kindness you showed me many, many years ago. Tomorrow a wild tiger will run loose through the city. I will be that tiger. However, no gunman nor bowman will be able to kill me. I am sure the king will offer a big reward to anybody that succeeds in getting rid of me. At that time, make yourself known and offer your services. Just take one random shot at me. You will be sure to hit me."

The student was astounded to hear this and quickly replied: "No, no! I can't possibly do such a thing. Just because of one little kindness, I cannot take your life."

"No, you mustn't think that way," the tiger said, still in the form of a young woman. "I am very old and just about ready to die. I have very few days left to live. Since that's so, it's my wish to show you my gratitude. Don't say another word—just do as I have told you."

The student would not listen to the tiger. "But how can I do such a thing? I cannot commit such a cowardly act just to win fame for myself."

Suddenly the woman flared in anger. "Why can't you understand?" she said. "By saying such things you are spurning my sincere feelings of gratitude. Cease your talking and do just as I have told you. Oh, one more thing—a number of people will be hurt. Go then to the Temple of Hungryung and ask for some bean paste. If you apply this bean paste to the wounds of the people, they will soon be healed."

She repeated her instructions and then faded away from his dream as the young student woke up.

He pondered this strange dream that he had had and waited in restless anticipation for the day to break. Sure enough, as dawn broke, a wild tiger appeared in the city and ran amok through the streets.

The capital was in an uproar. Bowmen and gunmen were dispatched to kill the tiger. But no matter how carefully they aimed their weapons, they could not hit the animal. The people were now in a terrible panic. Many had been hurt. Finally the king sent out a crier to announce a royal proclamation.

"Hear ye! Hear ye!" the crier cried. "The King proclaims that anyone who shoots the tiger shall be greatly rewarded. A high court rank shall be bestowed upon him and a great treasure of rice shall be his."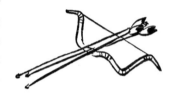

The student was surprised to hear this. A high court rank, and a treasure of rice—the rice alone would be enough to maintain a large retinue of retainers. And then he remembered the dream of the night before.

So the young student went before the king and said: "Don't worry, I'll kill the tiger!" The king gladly gave his consent for the student to hunt the rampaging animal.

The student went to the main street of the capital where the tiger was prowling about. Without even taking aim, the student took one shot at the animal. The wild tiger, that had the whole city in confusion, dropped dead.

That very day the student was made a nobleman and given his reward of a treasure of rice. He then got the bean paste from the Temple of Hungryung and applied it to the wounds of the people who had been hurt. Their injuries healed so quickly that his fame spread throughout the country.

Now, the story doesn't say so, but it is easy to imagine that the famous nobleman found for his wife the same woman whose shape the tiger had used in the young student's dreams—and that they lived together happily for many, many long years.

The Pumpkin Seeds

THERE once lived in the same village two brothers. The elder was greedy and miserly. The younger was a gentle and open-hearted man. The older brother lived in a great mansion and did not want for anything. Yet he was always complaining, as if by habit, that he led a hard life. On the other hand, his younger brother was poor and lived a humble life. But he never once complained.

One spring, swallows from some faraway southern country came and made a nest under the eaves of the poor brother's house. By the time the early summer breeze was rippling the green rice-seedlings, the swallow had hatched its eggs, and the nest was full of young birds. From morning to night, the baby birds made merry music under the eaves of the poor man's straw-thatched house. The kind-hearted younger brother placed a wide board under the nest to catch the baby birds, lest they fall from the nest to the ground below. The parent swallows busily carried food to their young and worked hard to help them grow big. And they did grow big, with each passing day.

One day, while the parent birds were away looking for food, a large green snake slid down the roof of the hut. As it approached the swallow's nest, it raised its head and peered inside, as if to say: "Yum, yum! These young birds should make good eating." The snake poised itself to strike, showing its fangs. Of course, the baby swallows had never seen such a horrible sight before. They flapped their small wings in fear and tried with all their might to fly from this unexpected danger. But their wings were too weak. One little bird succeeded in taking off only to crash to the ground.

The young brother heard the commotion and came running out of the house. He saw the snake just in time and, with a great cry, chased it away.

The bird that had fallen from the nest had broken a leg. "Oh, you poor little thing," the brother said, "it must be painful." He gently lifted the bird from the ground, set the broken leg and wrapped it carefully with a bit of white cloth.

Ten, then twenty days passed. The baby swallow with the broken leg was soon well again. It was strong enough to fly now. It no longer needed to wait for its mother to bring it food. It swooped through the great sky, swiftly and freely, in search of insects and bugs.

Summer passed and autumn came. The swallows left for their winter home in the south. The swallow with the broken leg was now a full-grown bird. Reluctantly, it too joined the migrating birds and left the village.

Early the next spring, the swallows came back to their old nest. They had traveled a long way, overseas and over mountains, but they had not forgotten their old home. The happy swallows swooped under the eaves of the straw-thatched hut. The humble hut of the younger brother again echoed to the chirping of birds.

The swallow that had broken its leg the year before also returned. As if to repay the young brother's kindness, it car-

ried in its beak a pump-
kin seed. The bird dropped
the seed in a corner of the
poor brother's yard, where
it soon sprouted and shot
forth a tendril that gradually climbed up to the roof
of the poor man's home.

By autumn, three big
pumpkins, so large that
each made an armful,
were ripening on the vine.
The younger brother was
overjoyed and picked one
of the pumpkins. "This
pumpkin alone would be enough to feed many people. I must
take some of it to the villagers." So he cut the immense pumpkin in two.

What should happen then! Out of the pumpkin trooped a
host of carpenters. Some carried axes, some saws, some planes,
and some hammers. Each carried some kind of tool. After the
carpenters had all come out, there came a flow of building ma-
terials—timbers, planks, window frames, and doors. In a twinkling of an eye, the carpenters built a large mansion and then
disappeared from sight.

The younger brother was completely dumbfounded at this
strange and unexpected happening. He then began wondering
what the other pumpkins might contain, so he gingerly cut open
the second one.

Out came a host of servants. There were farmhands too, with
plows and spades and rakes. There were also maids, carrying water jugs on their heads, and seamstresses, with needles in their
hands. When they had all come out, they lined up before the
younger brother and, bowing deeply, said together: "Master, we
are here to serve you. Please bid us as you desire."

From the third pumpkin there flowed silver and gold in such quantities that the younger brother was completely dazzled. Overnight, he became the richest man in the village, and soon he was the owner of vast lands, purchased with the money that had come from the third pumpkin.

The greedy elder brother was green with envy. His every waking thought was how to become as

rich as his younger brother. One day he came over to visit his brother, whom he had ignored for so long in the past. Slyly he asked: "Say, my dear brother, how did you manage to become so wealthy?"

The honest younger brother did not hide anything, but told everything that had happened.

The older brother, when he heard the story, could hardly bear his impatience. As soon as early summer came the next year, he took a baby swallow from one of the nests in his eaves and broke its leg. Then he set the broken leg, bound it with a piece of white cloth, and put the bird back into its nest. In autumn this swallow flew away to the south.

The older brother could scarcely contain his joy: "I've only to wait a short while longer. Then that swallow will return and bring me a pumpkin seed too."

Sure enough, the swallow whose leg had been broken on purpose returned the next spring to the elder brother's house. And sure enough, it brought back a pumpkin seed in its mouth.

The older brother took the seed and planted it in a corner of his yard. Every day he gave it water and cried: "Hurry and grow big! Hurry and grow big!" He did not forget to mix a lot of manure into the ground where the pumpkin seed had been planted.

In time, out came a green sprout. It grew and grew, stretching its vine up over the roof. In time, too, three pumpkins took shape and ripened. The pumpkins were much larger than those that had grown at his younger brother's house.

"How lucky I am!" the older brother said. "Thank Heaven! Now everything is set. I'll be much richer than my brother." He could not help dancing about in joy and anticipation.

Finally the time came and he cut the first pumpkin. But what should appear? Not carpenters, but a swarm of demons with cudgels in their hands.

"You inhuman and greedy monster! Now you'll get what you deserve!" the demons cried, and they started to beat and batter the brother.

After a while the demons disappeared. The older brother was all blue with bruises, but still he had not learned his lesson. "This time, for sure, I'll find much treasure," he thought, and cut open the second pumpkin.

But this time a host of money collectors came out, crying: "Pay your debts! Pay your debts! If you don't we'll take away everything we can lay our hands on."

And they did! They grabbed everything in sight. In a flash, the older brother's home was completely emptied of all it contained, leaving only a shell.

The older brother cursed himself for having cut open the second pumpkin, but it was too late. He could not give up his dreams of an easy fortune. He stuck a knife into the third pumpkin and split it open. What should come out but a flood of yellow muddy water. It came bubbling out in an unending stream. It flowed in such quantities that soon his home, his garden, and his fields were covered with yellow mud.

The older brother finally could stand it no longer. With a cry of anguish he fled to the shelter of his younger brother's house.

The kind-hearted younger brother greeted him with open arms and treated him with every consideration. The older brother suddenly realized how selfish and mean he had been. He became a humble and contrite man.

The younger brother gave his elder brother half of everything he had—paddies, fields, servants, and money—and from that time on the two lived on the most friendly of terms.

The Three Princesses

ONCE there was a king who had three daughters. All three of the princesses were gentle, noble, and beautiful. But of the three the youngest was regarded by all as the loveliest in the land. One moonlit night the three princesses climbed a small hill behind their father's castle to view the beautiful moon. Suddenly, a huge eagle swept down as if from nowhere and, in a flash, snatched the three princesses up in its giant talons. Then it rose into the air and carried them off.

The whole castle was thrown into turmoil. The king's bowmen and gunmen came rushing up the hill. But it was too late. The eagle was nowhere to be seen. All they could do was to gaze into the sky and bemoan the fate of the three girls.

The king's sorrow at losing all three of his daughters at one stroke was pitiful to behold. He immediately sent out his soldiers to proclaim throughout the land that anyone who succeeded in saving the three princesses would be given half his kingdom. In addition, he promised to give the savior of the girls his youngest and most beautiful daughter in marriage.

But who was there to save the princesses?

There was one, and only one, man in the whole country who knew where the maidens had been taken. He was a young warrior living deep in the mountains. This young man had left all human habitation behind and gone far into the mountain wilderness to perfect his martial skills. At night this solitary warrior used to mount his steed and practice with his spear and sword.

One night, as usual, the warrior had donned his armor and helmet and was spurring his steed in mock combat when he saw a huge eagle flying toward him. When it came near he saw, clutched in its talons, three young girls. By the light of the full moon, the warrior followed the flight of the great bird, and spurred his horse over hill and dale in pursuit. All night long he chased the giant bird, urging his horse on in pursuit, and, near dawn, he saw the eagle land at the base of a vast cliff and disappear from sight.

The warrior whipped his horse on, and after a time reached the spot at the base of the high cliff where the eagle had disappeared. Here he noticed a hole in the base of the cliff. This, the warrior thought, must be was the entrance to the Land-below-the-earth, a place he had heard about only in rumors. After carefully studying the entrance, the warrior was certain that he was right.

The warrior had also heard that in the Land-below-the-earth there lived a terrible ogre who slept, once he fell asleep, for three months and ten days. This ogre had many henchmen and kept a large number of eagles, which he used to steal treasures and kidnap people from the earth above. The warrior marked with care the entrance to the Land-below-the-earth and returned to his lonely home.

By next morning the story of the disappearance of the three princesses and the king's proclamation had reached even this remote part of the mountains where the warrior was in training. The young man set off immediately for the king's palace and was granted an audience with the ruler.

"O King," the young man said, "I shall bring back the three princesses."

The king answered: "Please do whatever you can."

The young warrior then asked the king for the loan of the five strongest men among the king's soldiers. Then he began preparations for his venture into the Land-below-the-earth. He prepared a rope a hundred leagues in length, a basket large enough to hold one person, and a silver bell. Then the young warrior set off for the mountains, accompanied by the five retainers.

After many days, he came once again to the entrance of the Land-below-the-earth. He tied the basket to one end of the rope and attached the silver bell to the other end. His idea was to lower the basket by the rope, and when the bell was rung, to pull it up.

The warrior ordered one of the soldiers to go down in the basket first. The man had gone down only one league when the bell rang "Tinkle, tinkle." The man was hauled up to the surface. He was white with terror. A second soldier went down as far as five leagues, but he too became afraid and was pulled back. A third, and then a fourth, was sent down, but each was overcome with fear part way down and had to be hauled out. Even the strongest of the soldiers, the fifth man, could only go down fifty leagues.

Finally the young warrior himself entered the basket and was lowered into the hole. Down, down he went. There seemed no end. Just as the hundred-league rope ran out, the warrior touched bottom. He had finally reached the Land-below-the-earth!

There he found thousands of large and small houses lined up, row after row. Among them he noticed one that was larger than the rest. It stood without any roof. "This," he thought, "must be the home of the ogre." The young warrior racked his brains for some scheme by which he could enter the house of the ogre, who was chief of the Land-below-the-earth.

As he approached the house, he noticed a well in the yard, and beside the well there stood a large willow tree. The warrior

climbed up the tree and carefully hid himself in the branches. Then he waited to see what would take place.

Soon a young girl came to draw water from the well. She filled her jug with water and lifted it in both hands to place it on her head. Just then the young warrior plucked four or five of the willow leaves and let them flutter down. The leaves fell into the water which had just been drawn from the well. The young girl emptied the jar and drew fresh water from the well.

The warrior again dropped leaves into the jar. Again the girl threw the water out and refilled her container. Once again the leaves came fluttering down, and once again the girl emptied the jar and refilled it.

"My, what a strong wind!" she said, and glanced up into the tree. At the sight of the warrior hidden there, she was startled. "Are you not from the earth above? Why have you come to this place?" she asked.

The warrior then told her how the three princesses had been kidnapped by a giant eagle and how he had been sent to save them.

The girl suddenly started to cry and said: "To tell you the truth, I am the youngest of the three princesses who were seized by the eagle. I was brought here with my two sisters. I had given up all hope of ever returning home. You cannot imagine how happy I am to see you. The ogre has just gone out. Once he sets out he does not return for three months and ten days. But, if we run away now, it would mean that the ogre would still be living, and, as long as he lives, he will try to steal us away again. You must wait until the ogre comes back and then get rid of him for good. But can you do that?"

"Yes," the warrior answered, "of course I can. That's why I came all this way."

"I'm glad to hear that," the princess answered. "Come, I'll show you how to get into the ogre's house."

The youngest princess then led the young warrior to the ogre's house and hid him there in the storehouse. In the storehouse, where there was a large iron pestle. The princess pointed to it and said: "Let me see how strong you are. Try and lift that pestle."

The young warrior grabbed the pestle with both hands, but he couldn't budge it an inch.

"At that rate, you'll never be able to take the ogre's head," the princess said. She went into the ogre's house and returned with a bowlful of mandrake juice kept by the ogre, and told the young warrior to drink it. He drank the juice in one gulp, and when he grabbed the pestle again, he was able to move it just about an inch.

The young warrior stayed hidden in the storehouse. Every day he drank mandrake juice and practiced with the iron pestle. Day after day, he tested his strength. Finally he was able to lift the iron pestle with one hand and fling it about as if it were a pair of chopsticks. But still the young warrior continued to drink the juice of the mandrake as he waited impatiently for the return of the ogre.

One day the ground began to tremble and the house started to shake. The ogre had finally come home, together with his many henchmen. They brought with them many treasures which they had stolen. When they finished carrying their spoils into the house, they prepared a mighty banquet. That night, they feast-

ed on delicacies of the
mountains and the seas
and drank wine by the
barrelful. All night long
they drank and danced,
and the warrior watched
them from a hiding place.

One by one the hench-
men went to sleep, com-
pletely drunk. The ogre
also finally toppled over
in a drunken sleep. He lay
snoring away.

"Now's my chance," the warrior thought and, drawing his
sword, crept up to the sleeping ogre. But imagine the warrior's
surprise! The ogre lay with his eyes wide open, although he was
snoring loudly.

The princess, who had followed the young warrior into the
room, then said in a small voice: "You don't have to worry. The
ogre always sleeps with his eyes open."

Then with a tremendous shout, the warrior slashed with all his might at the ogre's neck. The ogre jumped up, drew his sword, and tried to parry the blow. But the warrior's sharp blade had already bitten deep into the ogre's neck, and he could not move as quickly as usual. After repeated blows from the warrior, the ogre toppled over again. The warrior straddled the huge giant and finally succeeded in cutting off his head.

The severed head, however, tried to attach itself to the bleeding neck. Just then the princess took out some fine ashes of burnt straw, which she had kept hidden under her dress, and threw them over the stump of the neck. The head let out a loud moan. Leaping up, it then crashed through the ceiling and disappeared.

The ogre's henchmen, when they learned what had happened to their chief, all surrendered meekly. The young warrior then threw open the many storehouses of the ogre, each filled to brimming with gold and silver, and divided up the treasure among the ogre's henchmen. Then he gathered together the three princesses and returned to the place where the basket had been lowered.

The warrior pulled on the rope, ringing the bell at the other end. The king's soldiers, who had been waiting there all this time, started to haul away. One by one, the princesses were pulled up to the earth above. At the very end, the warrior also came up safely.

The king was overjoyed at the return of his daughters. He ordered twenty-one days of festivities to celebrate their new-found freedom from the terrors imposed by the ogre from the Land-below-the-earth.

The king did not forget his promise to the young warrior. He gave his youngest daughter, the most beautiful of the three princesses, to the warrior in marriage. He also gave the young man much land and wealth. The young warrior and his beautiful wife lived long and happily ever after.

The Signal Flag

ONCE upon a time there was an old man who was totally blind. Although he could not see anything, he had a strange power. He could perceive things which ordinary people could not. For instance, he could see the evil spirits that enter the bodies of men and women, making them ill or even bringing about their deaths. Furthermore, the old man knew the secret of casting spells over the evil spirits to make them harmless. Time and time again, therefore, the old man had saved men and women from the evil spirits that tormented them. He had saved hundreds of people and was famous throughout the land.

One day the old man was walking down a road, feeling his way about, when he felt a messenger boy pass by. And there actually was a messenger boy walking past him, carrying a great number of cakes in a box strapped to his back. The old man could tell that a small devil was sitting in the box with the cakes. The evil spirit, of course, was invisible to everyone but the old man.

"That little devil!" the old man thought. "He's up to some mischief. He plans to go into some house and cause trouble." So the old man followed the messenger down the road to a large house.

It was a house where a large wedding was being held. The boy entered the house and left the cakes that had been ordered for the wedding feast. The messenger then left after thanking the owners for their patronage.

The house was full of people, all in their fine clothes, gathered to celebrate this happy occasion. The old man waited outside to see what would happen.

Suddenly, there was a great commotion. The bride, who had been sitting in the inner room, had hardly taken a bite of one of the cakes when she fell to the ground and breathed her last. The evil spirit that had been sitting on the cakes had gone straight to the bride to do his mischief. The house was in an uproar, for, after all, one of the main figures in the wedding feast had passed away all of a sudden.

The old man immediately entered the house. "Don't worry," he said. "I shall save the bride for you."

The people immediately became quiet, because they knew this talented old man's reputation. In fact, there were even some among the wedding guests who had been rescued by him from evil spirits.

"The blind man is here! He can save the bride!" the guests cried joyfully. They were, indeed, so happy that it seemed as if the bride had already been restored to life.

Before the old man entered the bride's room to cast his spell over the evil spirit, he said to everyone present: "Close up all openings to the bride's chamber. Close the windows, the doors, the cracks, and the keyholes. Not a single hole, not even one as small as a pin-prick, must be left."

The people did exactly as the old man had said. They closed all doors and windows and plugged up all openings and holes they could find. After everything was ready, the old man entered the room and began praying. From the room came the quiet murmur of the old man's incantation.

In no time, there arose the sound of loud banging from within the room. It was the devil, feeling the torturing effects of the old man's spell. It writhed and it groaned as it struggled like a crazed beast to resist the old man's magic power. The devil's anguish was terrible to hear. The people outside thought the two were locked in mortal combat.

But this was not the case. The old man was simply sitting by the dead bride's side, with his hand on her forehead, intoning his curse in a low, quiet voice. The old man continued on and on, chanting his spell, gradually pressing the evil spirit to the floor.

Now, there was one young servant in the house who was not very bright. He burned with curiosity as he listened to the noise coming from the bride's room. Finally, he could no longer restrain himself. He crept up to the room and made a tiny hole in the paper-covered sliding door—a hole so small that only a needle would go in. Then the young servant peeked in.

But the devil had been waiting for something like this to happen. He saw his chance and, in a flash, slipped through the pinpoint hole and fled.

With the evil spirit gone, the bride came back to life and was greeted with joy by the wedding guests. But the old man was deathly white. He sighed and said: "Oh, what a terrible thing has happened! In just a little while I could have completed my spell, and the devil would have become harmless. But now the evil spirit is still at large. He is certain to revenge himself upon me.

I haven't much longer to live."

The parents and the wedding guests were overjoyed to see the bride alive again. Forgetting the old man, they crowded about her, all sharing their joy at her revival. In all this great fuss, the old man left the house before anyone had even thanked him properly.

Nonetheless, the old man's reputation grew, the story of his magic power finally reaching the ears of the king himself. The king, however, could not believe what he had heard and said: "It doesn't seem possible that a man who can't see people should be able to see devils and wicked spirits. He must surely be using some evil magic and fooling the people." The king then called his men and ordered them to bring the blind man before him.

When the old man appeared, the king placed a dead mouse before him and said: "Try and guess what I have placed in front of you."

"Yes, I shall. There are three mice there," the blind man replied.

"You'd be right," the king said, "if you said a mouse, but why do you say three mice?"

"I am certain that there are three mice," the old man countered. "There is no mistake about that."

"Quiet!" the king roared in anger. "There is only one mouse here. Are you trying to say that there is more than one mouse when I see only one with my good eyes?"

The king could not contain his anger and sternly continued: "You have fooled many people. You have committed a grave crime. In punishment, I sentence you to the extreme penalty. You shall have your head chopped off."

So the old man was handed over to the executioners and carried away immediately to the gallows, which lay on the outskirts of the city.

About to order the old man's execution, the king stopped and wondered: "He was able to tell that it was a mouse right away. Maybe it's not entirely false about his being able to see evil spirits. But I wonder why he insisted there were three mice instead of one?" The king, out of curiosity, had the mouse cut open. There to his surprise, he saw two small baby mice inside.

"This is terrible!" the king shouted. "Hurry and stop that execution!"

A retainer climbed the high castle tower and unfurled the signal flag. Now, it was the custom for the executioners, before cutting off a criminal's head, to confirm the sentence by looking at this signal flag on the castle tower. If the flagpole leaned to the right, it meant the criminal had been pardoned. If the flagpole inclined to the left, the execution was to be carried out as ordered.

The retainer lifted the flagpole and slanted it to the right. Just then, a sudden, strong gust of wind pushed the flagpole to the left. So strong was the wind that no matter how hard he tried, the retainer could not push the pole sideways to the right. The executioners looked up and, seeing the flagpole leaning to the left, went ahead with the sentence.

Just then, there was strange, crackling laugh near the flagpole on the castle tower. It came from the wicked spirit that had so narrowly escaped the old man's spell. He had taken his revenge!

The Magic Hood

THERE once lived a man who held his ancestors in great honor. The custom of the country was to have the names of the family's ancestors inscribed on votive tablets which were reverently set up in the family shrine. Then, whenever an anniversary of the death of one of the ancestors came about, the family would offer delicacies to the spirits of the dead and hold a ceremony in their memory.

Despite his reverence, this man had one weakness. He was not content unless his memorial ceremonies were more lavish than those of his neighbors. His weakness was to have so many different dishes of meat, poultry and fish that they could not all be placed on the table set before the votive tablets in front of the family shrine in the main room of the house.

The little goblins, who knew this man's weakness, decided one day to come and eat up the feasts the man would prepare for his ancestors. Each of the goblins had a magic hood which, when worn, made him invisible to humans. The next memorial day, the goblins came in their magic hoods and ate up all the delicacies the man had prepared. From that day on, whenever the man prepared a feast in honor of his ancestors, the goblins were sure to be there.

Of course, the man did not know what the goblins were doing. He was simply happy that his deceased ancestors were apparently enjoying their feasts so much. As this continued, the man began to increase the quantity of food and the number of dishes. But no matter how much food he prepared, it always disappeared overnight.

Finally, the man realized that even dead ancestors could hardly eat all that much. "There is something funny about this," he thought. The next time a memorial event came along, the man as usual set out many dishes on a table and placed it before the votive tablets. Then he got a long stick and hid behind a screen.

The hours passed slowly. It was the dead of night. Suddenly, the food started to disappear from the heaped platters set on the table. He listened carefully. From somewhere came the sound of eating and drinking. The man jumped out from behind the screen and started slashing the air above the table with his long stick.

The goblins were taken completely by surprise. They ran helter-skelter from the room. One of the goblins, however, could not dodge the stick fast enough. The end of the long stick caught a corner of his magic hood and lifted it from its head.

The man was surprised to see a red hood come falling from nowhere to the floor. He picked it up and placed it on his head and cried: "Robbers! Help! Help!"

His wife, who had been sleeping, came rushing into the room. But her husband was nowhere to be seen.

When the man saw the puzzled expression on his wife's face, he said: "The little goblins dropped this funny red hood."

But still the wife could not see her husband and looked around the room in bewilderment. The man went right up to his wife and then took off the hood. To her surprise, her husband suddenly appeared out of thin air and stood right in front of her.

The wife looked at the funny red hood which her husband showed her. Out of curiosity, she put it on her head. She too disappeared from sight. For the first time, they realized the magic virtues of the red hood.

"This is a wonderful thing we have gotten hold of," the man said. From that day, he put the hood on often and went out to rob people in their homes. He took anything and everything that pleased him. He stole many, many things from many, many homes.

One whole year passed in this manner. One day the man put on his red hood and went into a merchant's home. The merchant was in his inner room counting out silver and gold pieces.

Suddenly, the gold and silver pieces began disappearing one by one before the merchant's very eyes. "This is impossible!" the merchant cried. "It cannot be!"

Then he looked around the room. There, right in front of his eyes, he saw a small, thin strand of red thread dangling from nowhere, swaying back and forth. The man had used the cap so often that it had become ragged and had started to unravel.

The merchant quickly caught the thread and tugged at it. Off came the hood from the man's head, and there he was, complete-

ly visible to the surprised merchant. The merchant pounced on the man and started pummeling him. After taking the magic hood away from him, he then chased the man from his house.

The merchant then sewed up the ragged edges of the magic hood and, just as the other man had done, started wearing it to go out and steal.

One day he slipped into the house of a wealthy farmer. It was harvest time. The threshers were busy in the field threshing the new wheat. The merchant picked his way carefully through the threshers. By chance, one of the worker's scythes, lifted in mid-air, caught the corner of the hood, pulling it off the merchant's head. He was exposed to the full view of the threshers. The merchant was thrown into a panic and made a dash for freedom across the threshing floor. But the threshers, completely occupied with their work, kept flailing away, not even noticing the merchant. The merchant in his mad dash was hit on the head time and time again, until he fell unconscious to the floor.

The magic hood, which had dropped to the ground, was stepped on by the men harvesting the wheat. It was kicked about and crushed by so many feet that it soon became nothing but a dirty red rag, torn to shreds. And finally it disappeared altogether.

That was the end of the magic hood of the little goblin.

The Father's Legacy

ONCE there lived an old man who had three sons. In time he grew very, very old and lay on his deathbed. Just before he drew his last breath, he called his sons to his bedside.

"You have cared for me a long time," he told them. "I have only a few more minutes left to live. I want to give each of you a legacy, but, unlike in the old days, we now live in such poverty that I have nothing of value to leave to you. However, I want to leave at least something for you. When I die, you must leave this unfortunate house and try to find your own fortunes by your-selves." He then bequeathed the oldest brother a stone-mill. He left a long bamboo cane and a wine jug made from a gourd to his second son. To the youngest son he left a hand drum.

Soon, the old man passed away. The three sons grieved their father's death and honored him at the funeral. When it was over, they set off to find their fortune, each taking with him the legacy left him by his father.

After a while they came to a place where the road split into three. The three brothers promised each other that they would meet there again on an agreed-upon day and then parted. The oldest brother took the road leading to the right, the second brother took the middle road, and the youngest proceeded along the road leading to the left.

The oldest brother, carrying the heavy stone-mill on his back, walked on and on. As the road started climbing into the mountains, night fell. It was a lonely section of the country, where almost nobody ever came. The brother was hungry. On top of that, a cold wind had started blowing. He did not have the strength nor the courage to continue on.

"I wonder if there's some place where I can sleep," the brother thought. Just then he noticed an old tree in the distance. He decided he would spend the night under the tree and carried his heavy stone-mill there. However, he suddenly felt afraid.

"This is such a lonely place. What if some wild animal comes out at night?" he thought. He then again shouldered the stone-mill, which he had placed on the ground, and climbed with it up into the branches of the tree. There he hung the mill on a stout branch and settled himself to go to sleep.

It became completely dark. The night hours gradually passed. Tired from his long journey, the man was sound asleep. Suddenly he woke with a start. He could hear the sound of men talking nearby. Startled, the brother sat up in the tree and thought:

"What in the world could be happening in this lonely place, so far from any houses?" He peered down into the darkness and listened closely.

There, underneath the tree, he could just make out a band of robbers arguing over the division of the spoils they'd stolen that day.

"Your share is too large!" said one.

"No, my share is not enough!" said another.

Then they started to count their money. The older brother was amazed to hear the men counting in large sums: "One thousand *ryang*. Two thousand *ryang*."

The brother suddenly nodded his head as though he had hit upon a good idea. He drew his stone-mill to him and started to grind away. The stones began making a noise like thunder.

The robbers under the tree were startled out of their wits. "This is terrible! There's not a single cloud in the sky, but it's thundering. The heavens are angry with us. We shall be punished. Let's go! Let's go!"

The robbers scattered helter-skelter, leaving behind them the gold and the silver and the treasures that they had stolen. The oldest brother climbed down from his perch in the tree and gathered up the spoils the robbers had left.

Thanks to the stone-mill, the oldest brother became a rich man overnight and wasted no time in setting himself up in a splendid mansion.

The second brother walked on and on for days and days. One evening he passed by a lonely cemetery. Night had fallen and it was pitch-black. There wasn't a single star to be seen shining in the sky. The brother sat down beside a gravestone to rest his weary body, and waited for dawn to break.

It was just midnight when the brother heard the sound of footsteps from the other side of the dark graveyard. The footsteps sounded louder and louder as if the person were coming closer. It was so dark he couldn't make out who it was. He was so scared that he hardly dared to breathe and crouched against the gravestone, making himself as small as he could. The footsteps came right up the place where he leaned close to the stone.

"Hurry, hurry, Mr. Skeleton!" a voice said. "Get up! We have to do one job before dawn breaks. Tonight we're going to the home of a millionaire and steal his daughter's soul. Don't be so lazy. It's time to get up!" It was an evil spirit who had come.

When the brother heard the spirit's voice, he made up his mind in a flash and answered: "I've been awake for some time. Let's go then."

The evil spirit, hearing a strange voice, was puzzled: "Say, you sound like a human being. Are you really a skeleton?"

"If you don't believe me," the brother said, "then feel me."

The evil spirit stretched out his hands and groped in the dark. "All right then," the spirit said, "let me feel your face."

The young man thrust forward the gourd wine jug that his father had given him. The spirit felt the jug and said: "You're right! Your head hasn't a single hair on it. You must be a skeleton. But to make sure let me feel your arm too."

The second son then put forth the long bamboo cane his father had left him. The spirit felt the bamboo cane and said: "What thin bones you have! How dry they are! A long, long time must have passed since you died." Then the spirit added: "Hurry! Let's go! It will soon be dawn."

The spirit and the brother walked quickly out of the grave-yard and set off straight for the millionaire's mansion. When they got there, the house was in complete darkness. Not a person was awake. The spirit left the younger brother at the gate, saying: "Listen, Mr. Skeleton! You wait here. I'll go in by myself and steal the daughter's soul."

The spirit slipped into the darkened mansion. A little while later, it returned.

"Say, did you get the daughter's soul?" asked the brother.

"Of course," the spirit replied, "I plucked it right out of her. Here, I have it tightly held in my hand. This is the girl's soul."

"Why keep it in your hand? Put it in here," the second son said, hurriedly taking his draw-string purse from his belt.

The spirit put the soul into the purse and said: "Be careful now! Keep the purse tightly closed or the soul will escape."

The two then left the mansion and headed for the graveyard. Suddenly, in the distance, they heard the first crowing of a cock.

The spirit started with surprise when he heard the crowing. "This is bad," he said and ran swiftly away, back to the place where spirits stay in the daytime, when they must not expose themselves.

When day broke and the red sun showed itself in the east, the brother returned to the gate of the millionaire's mansion. He could hear the sound of people crying. The whole house was in an uproar.

"Did something happen?" the brother asked innocently.

One of the servants replied: "The daughter of the house suddenly passed away in her sleep last night. She had never been sick in her life and so, when she died suddenly, everybody was shocked beyond belief."

"Perhaps I can bring the girl back to life," the brother innocently suggested.

The servant, on hearing this, ran into the mansion. Soon the rich father came out to the gate and asked the young man in. "If you can really bring my daughter back to life, I will give you anything you desire. Please come have a look at my dead daughter," the father pleaded.

The old man then led the second son to an inner room, where the body of the daughter lay. The second son waved everybody away and commanded that no one enter the room. Then he shut the doors and the sliding windows tightly so that none could look in and went and sat beside the girl's body.

He took his purse out and, placing it close to the girl's nose, unloosened the strings.

The girl, who had not been breathing till then, suddenly turned over in her sleep. "My, I've overslept," she said and opened her big, beautiful eyes.

The millionaire's mansion, which until then had been filled with wailing voices, suddenly resounded with rejoicing. The father thanked the brother with tears of gratitude in his eyes. He bowed to the floor and kissed the young man's feet and said: "You are the savior of my daughter's life. No matter what I give you, I cannot repay you for what you have done. I believe you and my daughter must have been foreordained for each other from a previous life. I hope you will not take offense, but please take my daughter to be your wife."

The second son from that day on lived in the millionaire's mansion, as requested by the rich father. On an auspicious day picked by the soothsayers, the young man and the beautiful daughter were married. No man could be more fortunate than the second son, for not only did he marry an intelligent and virtuous woman, but he also received half the millionaire's wealth.

Thanks to his father's legacy, the second son was thus elevated in one day from poverty to wealth.

Meanwhile, what had happened to the youngest son?

Carrying the hand-drum left to him by his father, this brother walked on down the road leading to the left. By nature he was a carefree, happy-go-lucky man. He did not feel at all lonely, separated from his brothers. He traveled on and on for many, many days, until finally he saw in the distance a village set beside a beautiful forest.

His travels had not been in the least easy, but when he saw the beautiful scenery, he felt a strange feeling of elation. The brother started humming a song all to himself as he passed along a lonely path leading through the fields toward the village. He took down his hand-drum and began beating it in time to the tune he was humming. Then, caught in the rhythm of the drum he himself was beating, the young man started singing a song at the top of his voice as he walked on.

Suddenly, there appeared from the woods a large yellow animal which seemed to jog along in time to the song the youngest brother was singing. The young man looked closely, and, to his surprise, he saw that it was a huge tiger. Of course the young man was scared, but he kept right on singing and beating his drum. Soon, his fear disappeared as he watched the amusing way the tiger danced. The young man beat even more loudly on his drum. The tiger seemed overjoyed. It lifted its front paws off the ground, following to the brother's drumbeat. The young man kept right on singing and drumming away The tiger kept following him, dancing to the beat of the drum. On and on the two danced, drawing closer and closer to the mountain village.

When the villagers saw the huge tiger dancing behind the young man, they laughed and pointed. "That's something we've certainly never seen before!" They then started throwing money at the young man.

The young man saw what was happening, and he added a new verse to his song:

> *Come everybody, come one and all,*
> *Listen and heed this my call.*
> *Come see a tiger dance and prance—*
> *This is for you a lifetime's chance!*

After that, everywhere the young man went with his tiger

great crowds gathered to see the marvelous sight of the dancing beast, and money poured into the young man's pockets.

Eventually the story of the young man reached the ears of the king himself. The king said: "I must see, at least once, a tiger dancing to music. Go and bring the young man here."

The young man was led into the presence of the king, still playing his drum and still singing, with the tiger, of course, following him. When the king actually saw the dancing tiger, which he had only heard about till then, he could not help wanting the animal for himself.

"I'll pay you any amount you name," the king said to the young man. "Sell me that animal and drum."

"No," the youngest brother replied, "this is a treasure that has been handed down to me by my ancestors. No matter how much money you pay me, I can't part with my drum. And without it, the tiger won't dance."

In this way the young man declined the king's growing offers many, many times. But, after all, a king is a king, and in the end the young man could not keep on refusing. So he finally agreed to sell the tiger and the hand-drum for the princely sum of ten thousand *ryang*.

Thus the youngest son also came into great wealth, thanks to his father's dying gift.

On the day the three brothers had promised to meet, they gathered once again at the fork of the three roads. They told each other of their hardships they'd faced and the wealth they'd amassed. When each had told his story, the three brothers praised their father for the precious legacies he had left them. Each was now so wealthy that he had no reason to envy his brothers, and they lived on in peace and prosperity for many, many years.

The Silver Spoon

THE only son of a wealthy family had a tutor to help him in his studies. The tutor was a fine scholar, but he had only one eye and his nose was somewhat crooked. Because of this the servants of the house continually made fun of him. Even the food which the servants brought to him morning and night was not like that served the others. When he asked for anything, the servants would pretend they had not heard him. He would have to ask two or three times before the servants would do his bidding. The tutor was greatly troubled by the way the servants treated him.

But even more troubled was the young man of the house, the tutor's pupil. "I can't bear to see my tutor made fun of like this," he thought. "I've thought of a plan that will teach the servants a good lesson." The young master slipped quietly into the kitchen, so as not to be seen by the servants, and took from the kitchen cupboard his father's favorite silver spoon.

Next morning the servants were in an uproar. The kitchen

maids were white with fear. What would happen to them if the master were to learn of the loss of the spoon? The servants consulted a shaman. They also went to see a fortuneteller, to see if he might not tell them what had happened to the spoon and where it could be found. But neither were of any help. The servants searched high and low, turning the house upside down in the process.

The young son, with the most innocent expression on his face, casually asked one of the servants: "What's the matter? Everybody seems so upset this morning."

"Upset is not the word. The master's silver spoon is missing."

The youth suppressed his laughter and said: "Why, what a terrible thing! I wonder what could have happened to it?"

"If we knew, we wouldn't be in such a state now."

"That is bad." The youth was quiet for a while, as if in deep thought. Then he suddenly brightened, as if struck by a good idea, and said: "Hah! I know! My tutor is an amazing fortune-teller. He would surely be able to help you."

The servants had always made fun of the one-eyed, crook-ed-nosed tutor, but now they could do nothing in their plight but go ask him for help. The servants then did as the young master suggested.

First they served the tutor a special dinner with wine and the best of food to put the tutor in a good mood. Then the chief servant said: "The master's silver spoon has disappeared. Will you tell us where it is?"

"What? You say a spoon has been lost? H'm..." The tutor cocked his head in thought, while he held the wine glass to his lips in pleasure.

"Please," the servant implored, "you must help us! I am sure you can help us." And he bowed humbly many times before the tutor.

"Wait, wait. I shall try," the tutor said condescendingly. He sat down before his desk and pretended to be reading the future. After a while, he said confidently: "Well, well. The spoon is hidden quite near the house. Yes, it is under a stone that lies in a southeasterly direction. Let's see. A stone to the southeast? That must be the stones beside the well. Yes, that's it. If you look under the stones by the well, I am sure the spoon will be found."

The servants immediately went to the wellside and searched under all the stones. And there, sure enough, was the silver spoon. Of course, the spoon was found there. Everything had been planned long in advance by the youth. He himself had taken the spoon and hidden it under the well-stones. He had, of course, told the tutor of his scheme and where the spoon had been hidden.

But the servants knew nothing of this scheming. Instead, he earned their praise and admiration. The servants, who had been making fun of the tutor behind his back, now suddenly changed and began treating him with great respect. When mealtime came, the food served the tutor was much better than that served anyone else. Each time the servants brought in the food

on trays, the youth and the tutor would look at each other and smile quietly together.

All good things are followed by bad, so the saying goes, and in the case of the tutor a matter of great concern arose.

After the silver spoon was found, the story of the tutor's magic powers spread throughout the house. It finally reached the ears of the head of the house.

The young student's father, the master of the house, was a state minister in the king's court. At that time in neighboring China, the Chinese emperor lost his official seal. The whole country was in a turmoil. Unless the emperor recovered his seal, he would have to give up his throne to another man.

All the fortunetellers and the soothsayers in China were gathered together. Yet not one of them could tell who had stolen this valuable seal. A messenger was then sent to Korea who, after explaining the situation to the king, asked: "Please send us your very best soothsayer."

The king called his state ministers together to consider who should be dispatched to China. One of the ministers spoke up. It was the father of the youth who had hidden the spoon.

"We have a tutor who just recently located the whereabouts of a lost silver spoon. He is supposed to be a very famous fortuneteller. What about sending this tutor of mine?"

"That's most fortunate."

"Let's follow your advice." The other ministers of state all agreed to this suggestion.

The youth's father returned home and called the tutor before him. "It will be a hard trip, but I would like you to go to China on a mission," the minister said, and then he told the tutor in detail the story of the Chinese emperor's loss of his imperial seal.

"Oh, no! Not me. It's absurd!" the tutor said, and declined over and over again.

However, the minister had undertaken to send a soothsayer to China and he simply wouldn't take no for an answer. He was fully convinced the tutor was a great soothsayer. The greater a man, the more humble he is, the minister thought. Take this tutor for instance. Although he had the power to tell at one crack where the silver spoon had been hidden, not even once had he made known his ability. The tutor simply acted as any ordinary man would act. Thus, the minister was convinced that the tutor really was an extraordinary soothsayer.

"You don't have to be shy," the minister said. "Please do go. I beg you. There is nobody except you who can undertake this grave mission. Also, they say they will reward you with one hundred gold pieces. If you should succeed in finding the seal, imagine the honors that will be heaped upon you." So the minister was finally able to force the tutor to undertake this unpleasant mission.

The tutor did not care a thing about the reward of a hundred pieces of gold. But he could hardly bear the thought of the shame that would come to him when he was exposed. Of course, he thought, even if he could bear the shame, when they found out he had lied about his abilities, he would certainly be punished heavily.

"This is a terrible predicament," he thought, with pain in his heart. He went back to his room to ponder the difficult position in which he found himself.

A few minutes later, his pupil came into his room, all smiles. "You needn't worry, tutor," he said. "This is what I would do." Then the young lad put his mouth to the tutor's ear and began whispering to him in a very low voice.

The tutor kept nodding his head in agreement. The worried expression on his face gradually disappeared, and suddenly a cheerful smile lit up his features.

The tutor did not reveal his plans to anyone. He completed his preparations and then departed with the emissary from the Chinese court. The two crossed the Yalu River and entered China. When they reached the Chinese capital, the tutor was ushered into the emperor's presence.

In a voice filled with confidence he told the emperor: "I'll find the seal for you within three months, so please set your mind at ease."

The emperor was very pleased and answered in a cheerful voice: "I cannot thank you enough." Then the emperor commanded that the tutor be treated with all due respect and his residence be closely guarded lest any mishap overtake him.

Two months soon passed for the tutor, who was living a life of luxury and splendor. Each morning he went through his act of telling fortunes and divining the whereabouts of the seal. One morning, after going through the motions, the tutor sighed and murmured: "Oh, a terrible thing has happened."

Someone nearby who overheard his words asked: "What is the matter?"

"Oh, nothing to trouble you with. But last night a fire broke out in my house in Korea and burnt it to the ground. I don't care about the house, but the votive tablets of my ancestors were all destroyed too," the tutor answered, as if he had actually been at the scene of the fire.

"Can you tell such things too?" the person asked in surprise.

"Of course I can. If I couldn't tell such things, I wouldn't have come all this distance to look for the emperor's lost seal."

The tutor's answer was so surprising that the person was filled with doubt. Even if the tutor were the best fortuneteller under the sun, he surely wouldn't be able to tell of a fire which happened thousands of miles and to say that the relics of his ancestors were also destroyed. How could anyone believe such a thing?

The person went straight to the emperor and told him of the incident. The emperor decided to send a messenger to Korea. The messenger was dispatched ostensibly to extend the emperor's sympathies to the tutor's family. But, in truth the emperor wanted to find out for sure whether there had really been a fire on that day.

After a while the messenger returned with the report that there actually had been a fire on the very day the tutor had said. In addition, the messenger confirmed that the ancestral relics had also been lost, because the family had not been able to get them out of the house quickly enough.

When this news got around, everyone in the capital was deeply impressed. "The fortuneteller from Korea is really a remarkable man... He even knew of a fire that had taken place thousands of miles away... That isn't all! Once that fortuneteller gets started, they say he can foretell events that will take place a hundred years from now... Isn't he a remarkable person? He is sure to find the emperor's seal... They say he already knows who stole the seal. Well, we can look forward to seeing the robber executed soon..." Such tales spread quickly all over the city, with embellishments added here and there, until the capital buzzed with the supernatural powers of the wizard from Korea.

The fire had actually been planned between the tutor and his pupil long before. They had set a date for the fire to take place, and the house had been set on fire as planned. So there really was nothing to marvel at. But the people of China, of course, did not know this. They thought the tutor was a god and treated him as if he were one.

As the stories of the tutor's prowess spread throughout the country, the person most impressed was naturally the man who had stolen the emperor's seal. The person most impressed, he was also deeply worried. The tutor had said he would find the thief within three months. The thief now felt that he must do something quickly. He knew he would be found out sooner or later, with the all-seeing eye of the tutor reading into the hearts and souls of everyone. So the thief said to himself: "If I am to be found out eventually, I might as well give myself up now and ask for mercy. In this way I might at least save my life."

It was the next-to-last day of the three-month period the tutor had set for himself. A man slipped fearfully into the tutor's room. He was the thief who had stolen the emperor's seal. Making sure that no one else was around, the thief bowed low before the tutor and said: "Please spare my life."

His one eye flashing with anger, the tutor said: "You miserable fool! I was going to wait just one more day to see what you would do, and then I planned to go and tell the emperor your name. But now that you have come out and confessed your crime, I shall have pity on you and spare your life."

The thief was cowed by the solemn voice of the tutor, but with great relief he answered: "You will truly spare my life? Thank you from the bottom of my heart. The emperor's seal is hidden at the bottom of the pool in the middle of the Imperial Palace grounds."

"I knew that from before," the tutor said sternly. "I shall close my eyes to your crime this time, but you must never do such a thing again." The tutor then sent the man home.

Next day, the last of the three-month period, the tutor appeared before the emperor, who asked eagerly: "Have you discovered where the seal is hidden?"

The tutor answered: "Of course! Your worries are all over. I shall have it in your hands this very day. However, you must promise never to ask me who stole the seal. If you do, I will not be able to return the seal to you."

The emperor wanted the seal back so badly that he willingly agreed to the tutor's proposal.

"The seal is in the palace pool," the tutor said. "Please have the pool drained."

Immediately workers were set to work draining the pool. A thousand men busied themselves scooping out the water, and the bottom soon came into sight. And there the seal was!

Thus the seal was once again safe in the hands of the emperor. Thanks to the tutor, the entire country was freed from anxiety and fear. In addition to the promised hundred pieces of gold, the tutor was showered with many, many gifts.

His mission successfully completed, the tutor returned once more to Korea. There, his fame grew greater and greater than ever before. But his worries grew in proportion to his reputation. He could never tell when he would again be asked to tell fortunes or to divine secrets. Thus he was still in danger of being found out.

Once again, his pupil came up with a good idea. "Tell the people that you are sick, and stay out of sight for one month. After a month is over, tell them that you have recovered, but that because of your illness, you have lost all your powers of divination."

The tutor followed the youngster's suggestion and took to his bed. People kept coming from all over the country to ask for his help. But he refused to see any of them, saying that he was ill.

Then, blaming his illness, the tutor never again told any fortunes. As a result he was able to spend the rest of his life in peace, enjoying the great wealth he'd brought from China.

Land of Morning Brightness

TAN KUN, the Lord of the Sandalwood Tree, was the son of a spirit from heaven and a beautiful bear-woman. His father, they say, was Han Woon, the son of Hananim, the Lord of Heaven and Earth. When Han Woon came down to the Earth, he brought with him thousands of his spirit friends. Among them were the Lord of Winds, the Ruler of Rain, and the Driver of Clouds. He set up his court under a great sandalwood tree, where his followers remained spirits. They did not take on human forms like those of the wild people who then roamed over the land.

One day a she-bear and a tiger met on the side of the Ever-White Mountains, whose peaks hold back the clouds of the northern sky. As they talked, each beast declared that his greatest wish was to become a human being and walk up right on two legs. Suddenly a voice came out of the clouds, saying, "You have only to eat twenty-one cloves of garlic, and hide yourselves away from the sun for three times seven days. Then you will have your wish."

The tiger and the she-bear ate the garlic and crept out of the sunshine, far inside a dark cave. Now the tiger is a restless creature, and the wait seemed to last forever. At the end of eleven days he could stand the waiting no longer. He rushed out into the sunlight. Thus that tiger, still having the form of a beast, went off to his hunting again, on all four feet.

The she-bear was more patient. She curled up and slept the entire time. On the twenty-first morning, she left the cave, walking upright on two legs, like you and me. Her hairy skin dropped away, and she became a beautiful woman.

When the beautiful bear-woman sat down to rest under the sandalwood tree, Han Woon, the Spirit King, saw her. He blew his breath upon her, and in good time a baby boy was born to them. Years later, the wild tribes found this baby boy, grown into a handsome youth, sitting under that same tree. And they called him Tan Kun, Lord of the Sandalwood Tree. They made him their king, and they listened closely to his counsel.

The Nine Tribes of those times were rough people. In summer they lived under trees, like the spirits; in winter they took shelter in caves dug in the ground. They had not yet learned how to bind up their hair, to weave their own clothing, or to read and write. They knew nothing of growing good rice, nor of making savory kimchi. Their foods were the berries and nuts, the wild fruit and roots they found in the forests.

Tan Kun taught these wild people to cut down the trees and to open the earth to grow grain. He showed them how to cook their rice and how to heat their houses. Under his guidance they wove cloth out of grass fibers. They learned to comb their hair neatly, into braids for the boys and girls, into topknots for the married men, and into smooth coils for their wives.

Tan Kun ruled the nation wisely for more than one thousand years, when a second wise ruler arrived on the scene. This was the Emperor Ki Ja from across the Duck Green River, from

China beyond the Ever-White Mountains.

Tan Kun was no longer needed then, so he became a spirit again, and he flew back up to Heaven. An altar he built to honor his grandfather, Hananim, still stands on the faraway hills to the north."

This new figure of great importance was Ki Ja, often called the "Father of Korea." More than three thousand years ago, Ki Ja was an important official in China. He was unhappy under the wicked rule of the Chinese emperor who then sat on the Dragon Throne there. So he set forth to found a kingdom where people might live more safely and in peace.

Five thousand good Chinese accompanied Ki Ja, among them were doctors to heal the sick, and scholars to teach the ignorant people. There were mechanics and carpenters to show how cities could be built, and fortunetellers and magicians who knew how to keep away evil spirits. Books, paintings, and musical instruments were brought with them, also the precious worms that spin silk. Ki Ja gave his new subjects the Five Laws that taught them their duties to themselves and their fellows.

Those were golden days. Travelers were safe from robbers on the roads. Gates could safely be kept open after nightfall. Everyone was polite and kind to his neighbor.

Ki Ja's tomb could still be pointed out, not far from the Peony Mountain near Pyeng Yang, the capital city that was built by Tan Kun. The pillar of rock to which his first boat was moored still stood, but it too was outside the city gates. Pyeng Yang was built in the shape of a boat, so it was said. Now everyone knows a boat will sink if a hole is bored in its bottom. That is why it was forbidden in those early times to dig wells inside this boat city. That is why the people there had to carry all their water such a long way.

But what about Chu Mong, the Skillful Archer?

He, like Ki Ja, crossed the Duck Green River beneath the Ever-White Mountains. He, too, brought good ways to our land. In very early times, when Korea still was divided into many small kingdoms, there was a certain king to the north who wept because he had no son. One day during a hunt he knelt by a stream in the deep woods and prayed to the Jade Emperor of Heaven to send him a son. When he rose to his feet and turned toward his horse, he was startled to see great tears rolling out of the animal's eyes. The horse was pawing and pawing at a huge gray rock at the side of the path. Suddenly the rock moved, and the horse rolled it aside.

Beneath that rock, to the King's surprise and delight, there lay a small boy whose skin gleamed like gold. Because of this, and because of the fact that he had been lying under a stone, the King called the child Kim Nee Wa, or Golden Toad. And he cherished this son whom Heaven had sent him in such a strange way.

Now it was this same Kim Nee Wa who succeeded his father on the throne of that northern kingdom. And it was in his courts one day that an amazing event took place. One of his wives, sitting by a little stream in the garden, saw a tiny white cloud moving toward her. Gently it floated inside her dress, where it turned into an egg.

When the cloud egg was hatched and a fine baby boy was presented to the King, he grew very angry. "This child is surely the son of a demon!" he cried. "Throw it to the pigs."

But the fierce boars did not harm the child. They grew gentle as cooing doves, and they blew their breath on the baby to keep him warm through the night.

"Throw the demon child to the hunting dogs," the angry King cried. But again the snarling beasts became quiet. The dogs licked the face and hands of the tiny boy and warmed him with their breath.

"Put him amid the wild horses," ordered the King, for he feared this strange child. The wild horses also breathed softly upon the boy, and the mares fed him with their warm milk. "At, it's the will of the Jade Emperor of Heaven that this boy shall live," the King finally gave in. "His mother shall bring the child up as our son."

All marveled at the beauty and cleverness of the boy. From his shining face people called him Child of the Sun or Brightness of the Morning, which are just ways of saying Light of the East. Always kind to animals, he had a special gift for handling the horses in the King's stables, and he was made master there.

But, above all, people wondered at the boy's skill with the bow and arrow. At a young age, he could bring down a flying swallow. At fifteen he could slay a swift-running deer or pierce the eye of a wild goose flying high in the clouds. His like was not known on all the eight coasts. More often he was called Chu Along, or Skillful Archer.

Charming and handsome, skillful and kind, everyone in the kingdom preferred Chu Mong over all the King's other sons. Only his jealous brothers disliked him.

One day Chu Mong learned from his mother of a plot they were hatching to put him to death.

"You must flee, Skillful Archer. You must flee this night, my dear son," she warned.

With loyal friends at his side Chu Mong slipped secretly out of the palace. Under the light of the amber moon they galloped away south. When the morning sun gilded the peaks of the Ever-White Mountains, they were stopped by the deep duck-green waters of the River Apnok. They halted in dismay, for they could hear the sounds of the galloping horses of the pursuers.

"Listen, my friends," said the Archer. "Do you hear that? My brothers are coming. They are very near. I will call on the river dragon to help me." And drawing his bow he shot three of his arrows into the stream.

The river water then became pitch black instead of duck green. It was black with the backs of ten thousand fish. Squeezed tightly together, the fish made a firm bridge, over which Chu Mong and his companions easily crossed to the opposite bank. When the King's sons galloped up, the bridge of fish had once more floated apart, and Skillful Archer was safe.

Continuing on to the south, Chu Mong met friendly people. Three attached themselves to him to act as his guides. One wore the garments of the fishermen of this new land. A second was dressed like its farmers, or workers with tools. A third was clad in the embroidered robes of the officials. All welcomed Chu Mong and made him their king.

Skilled cavalrymen and archers were trained in Chu Mong's kingdom. Some say he invented the topknot as well as taught the people to eat politely with bowls, spoons, and chopsticks.

In his kingdom all lived in kindness and peace, and its ruler's fame spread abroad. Many years later to honor Chu Mong, his name, Light of the East, was given to the entire nation. So it is proudly called Chosun, or the Land of Morning Brightness.

Sticks and Turnips!

CHO always had good luck with his rice fields, so much so that he had huge chests filled with gold. But like many another fortunate man, he was not content with his lot. Cho grew tired of plowing his fields and harvesting the good rice. He longed for the softer, easier life of the capital city of Seoul.

"Now if I could only buy for myself an official's hat, I could grow even richer," Cho said to his family. Then as now, my children, it was always the government officials who grew rich. They handled the money the people paid in taxes into the King's treasury. Of course a good deal of that money went into their own brassbound chests. They called this their rightful "squeeze."

So this farmer came up to Seoul. He straightway sought out the Prime Minister to ask for a good position at the King's court. Cho made the Minister many rich presents. He went every day to the Minister's courtyard to plead his case.

"Perhaps tomorrow," the Minister said every time Cho laid a

gift at his feet. But that tomorrow never came. One year—two years—three years—and four. Again and again, Cho sent home for more money out of his chests. One does not eat for nothing here in the capital.

Then one day there came word that his chests were all empty. His rice fields were neglected. His house would have to be sold. His family were starving.

"Help me to the position now, Honorable Sir," Cho pleaded with the Minister. "My cash chests are empty. I shall have to give up and go home."

But the Minister only shook his head and again said, "Perhaps tomorrow."

Cho turned away from that Minister with rage in his heart. He vowed he'd get even somehow.

On his journey home Cho took shelter one night under the grass roof of an old country couple. They made him welcome. They shared their rice and their kimchi with him. They gave him the warmest part of the floor to sleep on. But as the sun rose and the cock crew, Cho, half-awake, heard them talking above him.

"It is now time to take the ox to the market," the old man said to his wife. "Get me the halter." And he began to tap Cho lightly all over his body with four little sticks. Cho tried to cry out, but to his surprise the only noise he could make was the bellow of an ox. When he rose from the floor, he found himself standing on all fours, and the old woman was putting a ring in his nose. As he went out of the hut, he had to make sure his horns didn't catch on the doorposts. The poor man had been turned into a great hairy ox.

As he was led along the highway by the ring in his nose, Cho's heart was filled with dismay at the trick that had been played upon him. He was the finest and fattest among the many animals at the cattle market, but his owner asked such a high price that at first nobody could afford the beast. Finally there came a butcher who had tarried too long in a wineshop. His senses were dull, and he paid the high price. Then he led poor Cho away to be killed.

Fortunately for Cho, the road they took passed another wine-shop. There the drunken butcher tied his prize ox to a stake, so that he might go in and have just one more bowl of *sool*.

Cho was hungry and thirsty too. And just across the road from the wineshop there was a field of fine turnips. With his great strength Cho was able to pull the stake out of the ground and to break his way through the roadside hedge. He pulled up a juicy turnip and sank his teeth into it. As he munched, Cho's hairy hide began to itch. His great body began to shake. He rose up on his hind legs. When he looked down at his hands and feet, he saw to his delight that he was a man again. Cho walked out into the road, where he met the drunken butcher, who begged him to tell him if he had seen his lost ox.

As Cho turned his face again towards home, he said to himself, "Sticks and turnips! Sticks and turnips! That is the secret. And if I can just get hold of those magic sticks, I can take my revenge upon that selfish Prime Minister."

Going back to the hut of the old country couple, he was welcomed as before. But this time, as soon as they were asleep, he began his search for the four magic sticks. Long before the sun rose and the cock crew, Cho crept out of the house with the sticks hidden in his sleeve. All his way back to Seoul, so he wouldn't forget, he kept saying to himself over and over again, "Sticks and turnips! Sticks and turnips! That is the secret."

Now Cho knew well the sleeping room of the official. The gates were unlocked, and the doors stood wide open. In the bright moonlight he had no trouble at all in creeping in to his victim.

With two of the little sticks he began to tap the sleeping Prime Minister. With wicked delight he watched the man's hands turn into hoofs and horns sprout from his forehead. But the Minister began to stir before Cho could use the other two sticks on his legs. He had to hurry away with his task only half done.

The next morning, as the sun rose, there was panic in the Minister's household. "Our Master can only bellow like an ox. There are horns on his head and hoofs where his hands should be.

His head and his shoulders are covered with ox hide." This awful news spread over the countryside like leaves in an autumn wind.

The servants summoned a famous doctor. He came in a chair on the shoulders of four men. But he could do nothing for the bewitched Minister.

They next sent for a sorceress, the most famous *mudang* in all the city. Out at the grave of the Minister's ancestors she wailed and she howled, she danced and she rolled about on the ground. She prayed and she prayed, but no help came to the Minister, who now was half ox.

It was then that the rice farmer Cho arrived once again at the Prime Minister's gate. He pretended to be surprised and shocked when he heard of the great man's curious plight.

"I can cure the Great Man," he said to the Prime Minister when the family led him in to see the the stricken official. "We had a case once like yours in my village. I surely can cure you, but the price is the position for which I have begged you so long."

The Minister bellowed consent, and the family promised that whatever Cho asked should be given him. Then the rice farmer went out to the market. He bought several turnips, which he dried in an oven until they could be ground to a powder. Everyone gathered to watch the Prime Minister lap up the turnip medicine with his great ox's tongue. There were cries of delight when the horns and the hoofs grew smaller and smaller. Together with the ox head and hide, they soon disappeared.

As soon as the Prime Minister was restored to his former self, he made his savior a rich man again.

Cho was given an important position at the court. He was granted the right to wear an official's hat with a jade button in his topknot and an official's gown, embroidered with a golden dragon. A tiger's skin covered the roof of his sedan chair. Fame and fortune were his, and all because of his finding the curious secret of the magic "Sticks and turnips!"

Why Dogs and Cats
Aren't Friends

A DOG and a cat lived in a small wineshop on the bank of a broad river beside a ferry. Old Koo, the shopkeeper, had neither wife nor child. In his little hut he lived by himself except for this dog and this cat. The tame beasts never left his side. While he sold wine in the shop, the dog kept guard at the door and the cat caught mice in the storeroom. When he walked on the river bank, they trotted by his side. When he lay down to sleep on the warm floor, they crept close to his back. They were good enough friends then, the dog and the cat, but that was before the disaster occurred and the cat behaved so badly.

Old Koo was poor, but he was honest and kind. His shop was not like those where travelers are persuaded to drink wine until they become drunk and roll on the ground. Only one kind of wine was sold, but it was a good wine. Once they had tasted it, Koo's customers came back again and again to fill their long-necked wine bottles.

"Where does Old Koo get so much wine?" the neighbors used to ask one another. "No new jars are ever delivered by bull carts at his door. He makes no wine himself, yet his black jug is never without wine to pour for his customers."

No one knew the answer to the riddle save Old Koo himself, and he told it to no one except his dog and his cat. Years before he opened his wineshop, Koo had worked on the ferry. One cold rainy night when the last ferry had returned, a strange traveler came to the gate of his hut.

"Honorable Sir," he begged Koo, "give me a drop of good wine to drive out the damp chill."

"My wine jug is almost empty," Koo told the traveler. "I have only a little for my evening drink, but no doubt you need the wine far more than I. I'll share it with you." And he filled up a bowl for his strange, thirsty guest.

As he was leaving, the stranger placed a bit of bright amber in the ferryman's hand. "Keep this in your wine jug," he said, "and it will always be full.'

Now, as Old Koo told his dog and his cat, that traveler must have been a spirit from Heaven, for when Koo lifted the black jug, it was heavy with wine. When he filled his bowl from it, he thought he had never tasted a drink so sweet and so rich. No matter how much he poured from it, the wine jug was never empty.

Here was a treasure indeed. With a jug that never ran dry, he could open a wineshop. He would no longer have to go back and forth, back and forth, in the ferryboat over the river in all kinds of weather.

All went well until one day when he was serving a traveler, Koo found to his horror that his black jug was empty. He shook it and shook it, but no answering tinkle came from the hard amber charm that should have been inside.

"*Ai-go! Ai-go!*" Koo wailed. "I must unknowingly have poured the amber out into the bottle of one of my customers. *Ai-go!* What shall I do?"

The dog and the cat shared their master's sadness. The dog howled at the moon, and the cat prowled around the shop, sniffing and sniffing under the rice jars and even high up on the rafters. These animals knew the secret of the magic wine jug, for the old man had often talked to them about the stranger's amber charm.

"I am sure I could find the charm," the cat said to the dog, "if I only could catch its amber smell."

"We'll search for it together," the dog suggested. "We'll go through every house in the neighborhood. When you sniff it out, I will run home with it."

So they began their quest. They asked all the cats and dogs they met for news of the lost amber. They prowled about all the houses, but they couldn't find a trace of their master's magic charm.

"We must try the other side of the river," the dog said at last. "They will not let us ride across on the ferryboat. But when the winter cold comes and the river's stomach is solid, we can safely creep over the ice, like everyone else."

So one winter morning, the dog and the cat crossed the river to the opposite side. As soon as the owners were not looking, they crept into the houses. The dog sniffed round the courtyards, and the cat even climbed up on the beams under the sloping grass roofs. Day after day, week after week, month after month, they searched and they searched, but with no success.

Spring was at hand. The joyful fish in the river were bumping their backs against the soft ice. At last, one day, high up on the top of a great brassbound chest, the cat smelled the amber. But, *ai*, the welcome perfume came from inside a tightly closed box. What could they do? If they pushed the box off the chest and let it break on the floor, the Master of the House would surely be warned and chase them away.

"We must get help from the rats," the clever dog cried. "They can gnaw a hole in the box for us and get the amber out. In return, we can promise to let them live in peace for ten years."

This plan was all against the nature of a cat, but this one loved its master and it consented.

The rats consented, too. It seemed to them almost too good to be true that both the cats and the dogs might leave them alone for ten whole peaceful years. It took the rats many days to gnaw a hole in that box, but at last it was done. The cat tried to get at the amber with its soft paw, but the hole was too small. Finally a young mouse had to be sent in through the wee hole. It succeeded in pulling the amber out with its teeth.

"How pleased our master will be! Now good luck will live again under his roof," the cat and the dog said to each other. In their joy at finding the lost amber charm, they ran around and around as if they were having fits.

"But how shall we get the amber back to the other side of the river?" the cat cried in dismay. "You know I can't swim." "You'll hold the amber safely inside your mouth, Cat," the dog replied wisely. "You can climb on my back and I'll swim across the river."

Clawing the thick shaggy hair of the dog's back, the cat kept its balance until they had almost reached their own bank of the stream. But there, playing along the shore, were a number of children, who burst into laughter when they saw the strange ferryman and his curious passenger. "A cat riding on the back of a dog," they laughed. "Have you ever seen anything so silly?" They called to their parents who joined them in their mockery.

The faithful dog paid no attention to their taunts, but the cat could not help joining them in the fun.

It, too, began to laugh, and from its open mouth Old Koo's precious amber charm dropped down into the river. The dog shook the cat off his back, he was so angry, and it was a miracle that the creature at last got safely to the shore. In a rage the dog chased the cat, which finally took refuge in the crotch of a tree. There the cat shook the moisture out of its fur. By spitting and spitting, it got rid of the water it had swallowed while in the river. The cat dared not come down out of the tree until the angry dog had gone away.

That is why the dog and the cat are never friends. That's also why a cat always spits when a strange dog comes near and why it doesn't like to get its feet wet.

The Tiger and the Puppy

ONE WINTER an immense tiger, strong enough to carry off a grown man, arrived in the village. And carry off a man it did, a man who was foolish enough to go out on the village street after night had fallen. Cows were not safe from that tiger, and pigs disappeared unless they were shut up tight inside the strong walls of the village courtyards.

"We need to set traps for Mountain Uncle," said the head official of the village. And they dug a pit at each end of the village street. Over these deep yawning holes they laid small logs and branches. They covered them lightly with earth and leaves, to deceive the great beast. When he walked across them, he would surely fall in.

But the tiger seemed to know about the hidden traps. He did not walk across them. Even when they were baited with live pigs, he did not go near them. Yet the village people could tell that he was out there. The head official himself was frightened almost out of his wits by the sound of that tiger clawing away at the grass thatch on his roof. Only by good luck and by shouting, and by beating on brass pots, did he succeed in driving the great beast away.

"We must call out the hunters from all the countryside," the village people said next. The tiger hunters came, in their blue uniforms and their red-tasseled hats. Their matchlock guns were slung over their shoulders. Their deer-horn cases were filled with bullets, and their oilpaper packets of gunpowder were safe and dry inside their sleeves. They did not forget to wind around their arms the long cords which could be fired to set the guns off. Walking swiftly and softly on their straw sandals, they started out for the hills.

The village official saw the hunters depart with relief. "Surely such a band of strong brave men would find the tiger. They would beat about in the bushes until they flushed him. They would wound him with their guns and finish him off with their spears. Then his precious soft skin would be the prize of the village official himself. The hunters could have the tiger meat to eat. He might also let them have the bones, teeth, and claws to sell to the medicine makers."

In Korea, in those times, powders made of tiger bones, tiger teeth, and tiger claws were highly prized. The warriors ingested these powders to give them strength and courage such as only a tiger possesses.

But the hunters came back empty-handed because they were afraid to go into the deepest parts of the forest. Or perhaps because this powerful old tiger was too smart for them.

"Let us put a new picture of this tiger in the spirit shrine outside the village," the people said. "Let's call on the spirit of Tu-ee, that great enemy of the tiger. He will help us drive him away."

That night, at the slightest sound, the villagers would run out into their courtyards, crying, "Tu-ee is coming! Tu-ee! Tu-ee!" But the bloody feathers of some chickens that had strayed out of their courtyard showed that the tiger had been there once again, despite their attempts to summon his spirit enemy.

The people were so frightened of the dreaded tiger that they all hid inside their houses at night. They shut up their animals, and when the orange and black beast stalked down the road, not a living creature was to be seen. Not one, that is, until on a certain night a foolish puppy left the side of its mother inside the stable and crept out to the gate.

It was winter, and the great tiger was hungry. When he saw the head of the little dog thrust through the gate hole, the beast licked its chops. With a bound he made for the hole, but it was, of course, far too small for him to force his huge body through.

Ordinarily, a tiger would not have bothered with a morsel so small as this puppy. Nothing less than a cow or a pig or a man would have attracted his notice. But the village folk had been so watchful that he had had no food in days, and his stomach was empty.

Lashing his great tail and snarling deep down in his throat, he fixed his flaming eyes on the mud wall before him, beyond which the little dog was hiding. The wall was high, and there were sharp, jagged rocks along its top. But the tiger thought he could leap it. Gathering his strength, he made one mighty bound. And over he went.

But the puppy wasn't there. With a sharp yip of terror the little dog had run out through the doggy door in the gate and into the street. The tiger could only see the tip of his tail.

There was nothing for the old tiger to do but to leap over the wall after him. With another great effort the orange and black beast made the high jump. But, of course, this time again he found no puppy there. The little fellow had wisely run back inside the gate.

As you know, there is no braver beast than a fierce tiger, nor one more stubborn. But the tiger's great head can hold only a single idea at a time, and this beast thought of nothing but of his own hunger. Over and over the high wall he leaped, over and over, until at last his strong heart gave out.

The next morning, the villagers found the tiger lying dead outside in the street, and the little puppy fast asleep in the hole in the gate.

The Bird of the Five Virtues

A MAN once came across a goose. Thinking to gain favor, he made a present of the goose to the Governor of his province. The official grew fond of the bird, putting it in the garden and ordering the servants to feed it the best grain.

One day as the Governor walked in his garden, a servant addressed him. "Honorable Sir," he said, bowing low, "that fat wild goose would make a very fine feast. Its flesh is sweet and tender. Its flavor is fine. I pray you, kill it and eat it."

"Kill a wild goose and eat it?" the good Governor replied. "Never! The wild goose is the bird of all the Five Virtues, *In-eui-ye-chi-shin*."

"How could that be, Honorable Scholar?" the servant asked. "How could a bird know about the Five Virtues?"

"Think, Man!" the Governor said. "First, the wild goose is an example of love. It does not fight like the eagle nor hunt like the falcon. It lives in peace and friendship with its fellows.

Second, when it takes a mate, it observes all the rules of right living. And when its mate dies, the goose mourns her loss like a true wife. She comes back again and again to her former nesting place, alone and a widow. What wedding in our land is complete without the wild goose as a symbol of devotion?

"No, my good man, I should not wish to kill a bird with such a fine character. Watch the wild geese, how they fly. In order, and with ceremony, they make their procession across the blue sky. And what wisdom they show, seeking the warmth of the south in the cold winter and the cool air of the north when the hot summer comes!

"You have seen for yourself, how they come back to our north country every year at the same time. Thus they keep the faith. *Ai*, the wild goose lives by the Five Virtues. So who would destroy so noble a bird?"

The Blind Man's Daughter

IN A beautiful little village lived a girl named Sim Chung. Her mother was dead, and her father was growing blind. Chung was the one treasure of that poor man. Her face was smooth and white, like a piece of ivory carving. Her brows had the curves of a butterfly's wings, and her hair shone like the lacquer on the shining black table in Ancestors' House. In all her life no illness had ever befallen Chung. Not even the Great Spirit of Smallpox had been able to harm her.

Chung was as good and kind as she was fair and wise. She never wasted anything, not a grain of rice nor a piece of kimchi. She guided her father's faltering steps, but with his blindness the poor man no longer could work. Their possessions had to be sold, one after another, to keep them alive.

When the girl reached adulthood, it was no longer proper for her to accompany her old father on the street. So the blind man crept off alone, begging for change from the passers-by.

One day he stumbled into a ditch. While he was trying to climb out of it, a firm hand lifted him up, and a voice spoke to him, "Give me three hundred bags of rice for the temple, Old Man, and in time your vision will be restored." Sim marveled at these words. When he found that the speaker was a priest from the temple on the mountain nearby, he believed the man's promise and hope filled his heart.

But when he repeated it to his daughter, sadness swallowed his hope.

"*Ai-go! Ai-go!*" he wailed. "There is no way for beggars like us to obtain so much rice."

But in a dream that night, Sim Chung's dead mother told her how she could obtain the rice that would restore her father's sight. The next morning the good daughter disguised herself in the big hat and the long coarse gray gown of a person in mourning for the dead. She covered her nose and her mouth with the thin white-cloth shield a mourner always carries before his face. In her clever disguise, she made her way to a rich merchant's courtyard.

This man owned many boats which carried cargoes of rice to faraway China, but of late the River Dragon had barred his way by churning the water into dangerous waves. The toll for safe passage which the Dragon demanded was a beautiful girl. The merchant had offered no less than three hundred bags of rice to the young woman willing to offer herself as a sacrifice.

The merchant grew sad when he heard Chung's story. "So dutiful a daughter," he said, "does not deserve to die." But there was no other way for her to get the rice, so the bargain was made.

Chung's heart was glad when she watched the long line of horses, carrying the bags of rice to the priest's temple up in the hills. But her heart was sad when the priest told her it might take many years for her father to see again.

The girl bowed before the tomb of her mother and prayed her to send heavenly spirits to care for the old man until he should be cured. She also asked their kind neighbors to watch over the old man. Then she set forth to keep her part of the bargain she had made with the merchant.

When she was dressed for her journey to the Dragon's watery realm, Chung shone brighter than the sun in the eastern heavens. Wearing a bride's green gown, with jewels and bright ribbons in her wedding headdress, she rode at the head of the merchant's procession of rice boats. Soon they came to the place in the river where the Dragon barred the way with the lashings of his great tail. To save this poor girl, the merchant offered to give many bags of his rice to the river spirit. All on the boats wept for their hearts were touched at her great love for the blind father. But the River Dragon would not be satisfied by any substitute for Chung.

So the girl bowed to Heaven and jumped off the side of the boat. The angry waters grew as calm as those of our garden pool. The boats passed safely across them and went on their way to the Flowery Kingdom of China.

Whether the fish whisked her along on their fins or she was carried by the dragon servants of the Sea King, Chung never knew. She found herself floating between waving undersea plants, amid bright-colored fish. She caught glimpses of pearls as big as your fist and of walls of black marble. Then she was led into the palace of the Sea King himself.

The bewildered girl bowed before this Jade River Dragon, and said, "Honorable sir, I am only the daughter of the blind beggar, Sim. I'm not worthy to come before one so exalted as you."

But the Sea King replied, "The light of the stars finds its way down to our undersea kingdom, and a message about you has come to us from Hananim, the Emperor of Heaven and Earth. You will be well rewarded for your goodness to your blind father."

Sea maidens dressed Chung in fine robes. They spread out before her soft sleeping mats, and gave her tasty treats. In this life of comfort and ease, the girl grew more beautiful than ever before.

One day her attendants led Chung to a giant lotus blossom that lay on the river bottom. It was so large that they could hide her away within its fragrant heart. The Sea King bade her farewell, and the girl felt herself rising up through the water. Soon, to her amazement, she saw the lotus flower was floating on the river, close to the boat of her friend, the rice merchant.

"Never in Heaven or on earth was there such a lotus flower as this," the boatmen said to the merchant. "It must go to the King." They were richly paid for it, and the King treasured none of his possessions so much as this rare, giant blossom. He went daily to see it in the special garden pool it floated on.

Only at night did Chung come out of her hiding place in the giant flower. Somehow its perfume served her as food, and the dew on its petals quenched her thirst.

In the moonlight one evening the King came upon the girl as she walked on the bank of the crystal pool.

Modestly she turned to hide herself from his sight, but her lotus-blossom shelter had vanished. The King was afraid at first she might be a spirit, but her beauty delighted him. The wise men who studied the heavens declared that on the day the lotus flower was brought to him by the boatmen, a bright new star had appeared overhead in the sky. With this good omen to reassure him, the King made Chung his wife.

Chung was elated, as who wouldn't be if she'd just been made a queen? But there were times when her heart also was sad. She thought often of her poor father, whose eyes were no doubt still closed to the world about him. One day her husband, the King, came upon her crying as she sat in the garden.

"*Ai-go*, great and excellent one," Chung said to the King when he asked why she wept. "It is a dream I have had about a blind man. His plight touches my heart. I should like to do something for all the blind in your kingdom. I should like to give them a fine feast."

One day, two days, and three days, the blind beggars of the land came to eat rice and kimchi in the King's courtyard. Peering at them through curtains, Queen Chung had hoped one of them would be her father. But the end of the feast came without Sim's appearing. The servants were just turning away a latecomer when the Queen recognized him through his tatters. She gave a loud cry. "*Abuji! Abuji!* It is my dear father."

They dressed Sim, the blind beggar, in new clothing and brought him into the Queen's chamber.

"What wonder is this?" said the blind man when he heard his dear daughter's voice. "Do apricots bloom in the snow? Do horses have horns? Do the dead come to life? How can I be sure you are truly Chung unless I can see?" The old man rubbed his dim eyes, and suddenly, as the temple priest had foretold, his sight returned.

When the King heard the tale, he heaped honors upon the father of his beloved Queen. He gave him a fine house. He appointed him to a high position at court. He even found him a wife.

Now Queen Chung's happiness was complete. The Sea King's promise of a heavenly reward for this dutiful daughter had been fulfilled.

The Man Who Lived
a Thousand Years

SOME say Tong Pang Suk lived ten thousand years, while others claim that was far too long. He most certainly had lived a thousand years though. Someone had been careless in the Heavenly Emperor's Hall of Recording. There were kept the Books of Life in which all people's names are recorded, so that, so that the judges can determine the time for each one to be brought to the Jade Emperor's Heavenly Kingdom.

Perhaps it happened that the pages for Tong Pang Suk were stuck together, or perhaps the judges turned them too fast before the book was put away behind the panels. But, whatever the reason, that old man's name was overlooked and no messenger was sent to take his spirit away from the earth.

Even when Tong had lived out the full course of a man's life, no summons came. What could he do? He grew no older, for he was old as a man could be. He simply lived on and on, one hundred, two hundred, three hundred years.

His childhood friends, long since departed to the Distant Shore, missed their old neighbor Tong. "How is it?" they said to one another, and to the Jade Emperor as well. "How is it that Tong Pang Suk remains so long on the earth?" One hundred, two hundred, three hundred years more it was before his pages in the Book of Life were found, and a messenger was finally sent to bring Tong Pang Suk up to Heaven. That messenger was a spirit, of course, but he took on the form of a man. Like Chung, the blind beggar's daughter, he disguised himself as a mourner. Hidden under his great hat, he wandered over the earth, looking for Tong.

By this time Tong had become used to his great age. His days were calm, without wind and without cloud. And he spent most of them on the bank of a stream lost in the pleasures of fishing. The old man had no wish to die. His greatest fear was that the Heavenly Messenger might one day catch up with him. Each sixty years he took on a new name and moved to a new village so that he could not be traced. But always he fished.

Somehow the Spirit Messenger heard of this old, old man who sat, always fishing, on a river bank. He thought perhaps this might be the one he was looking for, so he set a trap for him. Not far from where Tong fished, the Spirit Messenger threw several bags of charcoal into the river. Its black dust clouded the water so that it looked like ink paste.

"Why did you do that foolish trick?" Old Tong inquired when he found the source of the blackness that was spoiling his fishing.

"Honorable grandfather, I'm just washing my charcoal. Soon it will be as white as the jacket you're wearing," the Spirit replied.

"*Ai! Ai*" exclaimed Tong, shaking his head. "I've lived here for nine hundred years, but never before have I met a man foolish enough to think he could wash black charcoal white."

The Spirit was happy now, for he knew he had found the man he was seeking. He followed Old Tong wherever he went, hoping for a chance to carry him off to the Other World. So close did he keep to the old man's heels that Tong Pang Suk guessed

who he might be.

"You are brave, learned sir," Tong said to his spirit companion one day. 'The country roads here are dangerous. Aren't you afraid traveling such unfamiliar routes?"

"I'm not afraid of country roads," replied the Spirit who, in truth, was not nearly so quick-witted as Tong. "There are but four things on this earth that I greatly fear, and wherever they are, there I am not."

"What are the four things the Great Man fears?" Tong asked politely.

"A branch of a thorn tree, the shoe of an ox, foxtail grass, and a salt bag. Those four put together would bring me to my doom."

"And you, venerable father," the Spirit asked in his turn, "what do you fear the most?"

Now Tong, being crafty and wise, quickly replied. "The things I fear most of all," he said to the Spirit, "are roast suckling pig and the beer called *mackalee*."

Suddenly beside their path Old Tong saw foxtail grass growing beneath a thorn tree. By the side of the road near it he found a castoff straw ox shoe and an old empty salt bag.

Gathering up the shoe and the bag, the old man quickly left the road and took refuge beneath the thorn tree. He plucked a thorn branch from over his head. He gathered some foxtail grass from under his feet. Thus quickly he completed the charm, and he tied all four parts of it into a bundle.

From a safe distance the unhappy Spirit begged the old man to leave the safety of the thorn tree. He wept and he raged, but he dared not approach because of the charm. Then the Spirit remembered Old Tong's words about the things he feared most. He went off to the village and fetched a roast suckling pig and a jug of *mackalee* beer. These he flung at Old Tong, hoping to drive him out of his refuge. Instead, to his amazement, the Spirit saw the old man eating the roast pig with great gusto and drinking the mackalee beer with delight. He shook his head in bewilderment, and he gave up his idea of whisking Tong up to Heaven that day.

But the Spirit Messenger was not yet beaten. He did not fly back to Heaven and give up his quest. For a hundred years more he waited and watched, hoping Tong would forget to carry with him the bundle he had made of the thorn wood and the foxtail grass, the ox shoe and the salt bag.

At last the Spirit Messenger's patience had its reward. One day the old man did forget his charm as he set forth to fish, and the Spirit carried him off to the Heavenly Realm.

Since then, all people who know the secret of Tong and his charm use it to protect themselves from evil spirits. It doesn't keep them from going to the Heavenly Kingdom when their time comes, but it drives many bad spirits away from their courts.

A Fortune from a Frog

A POOR couple lived in a hut in the Diamond Mountains. They were both unhappy because there was no son under their grass roof to pray for their spirits when the time came for them to exit through the Earthly Gates. They were too poor to adopt a boy to bring up as their son, who might perform this service for them.

Their fields on the mountain sides gave this couple only enough rice to keep them alive. The cabbage, turnips, and peppers they could raise in their rocky garden made only enough kimchi for their own consumption. They had hens which laid a few eggs, and they found honey in the nests of the wild bees in the rocks. So they did not starve.

For buying their clothes and their salt they depended on the fish which Lah caught in the nearby mountain lake and which he sold in the village in the valley below. So you can guess how distressed he was when, one morning, he saw that his lake had dried up and the fish had all disappeared. On the bank sat a giant frog, as big as a man. It was just finishing drinking up the lake water.

"Wicked frog," poor Lah scolded. "What demon possessed you to drink up my lake and to devour my fish? Have I not enough trouble without such a disaster?"

But the frog only bowed politely and replied in a soft voice, "Honorable sir, I, too, regret the disappearance of the lake, for that was my home. Now I have no shelter. Pray give me refuge under your roof."

At first, Lah refused, as he had good reason for doing. But the gentle words of the frog softened his heart. His wife also objected when her husband led the giant frog into their hut. But it was lonely there on the mountain side, and the woman was interested in the fascinating tales the frog told. She brought in leaves to serve as his bed, and she thoughtfully fetched water to make it comfortably damp to suit a frog's taste.

Early the next morning, Lah and his wife were wakened at dawn by the sound of loud croaking. The din was as great as that of soothsayers trying to drive evil spirits from the stomach of a sick man. Hurrying out on their veranda, they saw the giant frog lifting his croaking voice to the heavens. But their eyes soon turned away from the reddening eastern sky to the shining treasures they saw in their courtyard.

Our New Year gifts could not compare with those the frog had provided for his good hosts. There were strings upon strings of copper, and valuable silver coins, too. There were fat bags of rice, great jars of kimchi, packets of seaweed, and delicious salt fish. Piled beside were rolls of silk and cotton cloth, hats, padded stocking, quilted shoes, fans, pipes and stunning silver and gold ornaments. The frog had gifted them with a fortune!

In the fine sedan chair the frog gave her, Lah's wife journeyed to the inner courts of the valley houses. She made friends with the women there, and from them she learned more and more about the people of that neighborhood.

"Tell me about Yun Ok," the frog always asked when the

woman returned. Yun Ok, or Jade Lotus, was the youngest daughter of the richest *yangban* in all that northern province. She was, so the gossip of the inner courts had it, by far the most beautiful girl in the land. Her skin was like a pale cloud. Her eyes and her hair were as black as a raven's wing. Her form was as graceful as bamboo bent by the spring breeze.

"It is Yun Ok I must marry, Omoni," the frog said to Lah's wife, whom he now was permitted to think of as his mother. "Go, honorable Lah, go now and ask for Yun Ok for my bride."

"No way!" Lah snapped back. He trembled at the thought of asking the great *yangban's* daughter to marry a frog. But the golden words of the frog persuaded him. He went, wearing such elegant clothing that the servants of the *yangban* swiftly admitted him to his Hall of Guests.

The family's two older daughters had married disappointing young men, and the proud father of Yun Ok was determined his youngest daughter should have a better husband.

"Is this suitor rich?" he demanded of Lah. "Yes, great sir, he is rich."

"What kind of jade button does he wear in his hat?" he inquired, which is the same as to ask what government office he holds.

"Well," said Lah, "that I cannot exactly say."

"Is he handsome? What is his name?" All these were the questions the father of a daughter always asks of a go-between who comes to arrange a marriage.

"You could not call him handsome, I think," the poor man replied. "And his name? He's called Frog, because that's what he is, a frog. But he's as large as a man, and golden words come from his mouth."

"A frog! This is an insult! Bring out the paddles," the angry *yangban* shouted. Unlucky Lah was seized and laid down on the ground, ready for a severe paddling. The servants raised the dreaded clubs with their hard, flattened ends. They were about to give Lah a terrible beating when dark clouds covered the sun. Lightning flashed. Such terrible thunder was heard that the men dropped their paddles in terror. Only when the *yangban* gave orders to untie Lah did the sun fill the heavens and earth with bright light again.

"This is surely a sign from the Jade Emperor of Heaven," the *yangban* said sadly, and he consented to the marriage of his daughter, Yun Ok, to the frog.

That must have been a curious sight, a giant frog sitting on the white horse of a bridegroom. Of course the bride could not see it, for according to custom her eyes were sealed shut with wax. It was not until the wedding feast had been eaten that Yun Ok found out she had married a giant frog.

"Don't cry, Yun Ok," her strange new husband offered as comfort. When they were alone in the bridal chamber, he gave her a sharp knife to slit his frog's skin up the back. When he wriggled out of the skin, a tall and handsome young man stood before her. Wearing a silk robe and a jade button in his topknot, he was a *yangban* of the *yangbans*. He explained the strange happening thus:

"I am the son of the King of the Stars. My father, being displeased with some of my actions, decided to punish me. He sent me down to the earth in the form of a frog, and he commanded me to perform three unheard-of tasks. First, I was to eat all the fish in a lake and to drink its waters dry. Second, I must persuade a human couple to adopt me, a frog, as their son. Third, I must marry the most accomplished woman in all the land. Only then could I return to his starry kingdom. Those three tasks have been done. But the hour of my return is not yet. When I do go, Yun Ok, I will take you to dwell with me in the sky."

The delighted bride sewed her handsome husband back into his frog's skin, and he went off on the journey a bridegroom always takes after the wedding, otherwise people would think he like his new wife too much. While he was gone, Yun Ok only smiled when her sisters and their foolish husbands made fun of her frog.

Her *yangban* father, although he had given consent, was not pleased with the marriage. His sixty-first birthday was near, and as everyone knows, that is the most important occasion in any man's life. All members of his family were invited to a great feast—all, that is, except his frog son-in-law. To provide the food for the feast, his other two sons-in-law were sent out to hunt game and to bring fish from the rivers and lakes.

When the frog heard of the feast, he went to see the king of the tiger clan. "Take all the wild beasts, both little and big, into your cave," he said. "Hide them all from the hunters!" He likewise summoned the king of the fishes and gave him the command to hide all the finned creatures on the bottoms of the rivers and lakes. So there was no game for the hunters, no fish for the fishermen, and no food at all for the birthday feast.

The *yangban* was dismayed. But as he wrung his hands over his plight, the largest procession ever seen streamed through his gates: horses carrying wild boars, tender young dear, fish of all kinds, wild ducks and more game than the guests could possibly eat.

At the head of the procession was a chair covered with tiger skins and carried by sixteen men. A bright-faced young man rode inside. The *yangban* was startled to learn that the shining Prince was in truth his youngest daughter's despised husband, who had worn the frog's skin.

The *yangban* bowed before the Star Prince, although that is not the custom between a man and his son-in-law. He begged forgiveness for his neglect, and he offered the frog-husband the seat of honor at the feast.

But the Star Prince simply told his wife to get ready for their journey and a great cloud from Heaven lifted them up to the sky. That night the wise men who study the heavens found two new stars shining brightly just overhead. What else could they be but the fair Yun Ok and her frog, the son of the Star King?

The fortune brought to Lah by the frog lasted throughout his whole life. His riches grew ever greater and greater, he wore the jade button in his official hat and it was New Year in his court all year long.

A Korean Cinderella

NAN Yang was the daughter of a village official. When her mother died, her father married a mean woman with two vain, selfish daughters.

These three wretched women had no love for that poor motherless Nan Yang. They made her work from the first light of the dawn to the coming of dark, and even far, far into the night. She had to clean the rice and fetch the water. She had to gather firewood for the hungry mouth of the stove and swept the courtyard, all by herself.

Instead of using her own name, Nan Yang, or Orchid Blossom, they nicknamed her her Dirty Pig. They were always coming up with new ways to humiliate the girl and make her cry.

When her other work was at last done, they gave her the ironing sticks. To the sound of her pounding, these three selfish creatures fell asleep night after night. Nan Yang's father could do nothing, for he feared the sharp tongue of his new wife, as much as the poor girl.

That summer, a fair was coming to their country villlage. All the people were going—to hear the musicians, to see the comic acrobats, and to listen to the captivating tales of the traveling storyteller. There would be candy and cakes and other strange foods to buy.

"You may go to the fair, Dirty Pig," the unkind stepmother said to Nan Yang, "but only when you have husked this sack of rice, and only when you have filled this cracked jar with fresh water."

Nan Yang's father, wearing his new hat and best long white coat, looked very sad. But he dared not oppose his meanspirited wife. Poor Nan Yang wept as she watched them all depart for the fair, and she envied her stepsisters in their pretty new dresses of bright pink and green.

With a sigh the sad girl began the tasks her stepmother had set her. But she had scarcely poured the sack of unhusked rice out on the ground when there was an odd swishing noise and a deafening twittering. These strange sounds came from the wings and the throats of ten thousand little birds landing on the immense pile of rice. With their tiny sharp beaks the birds pecked off the husks. Almost before Nan Yang could dry her tears, the rice grains were white and clean. She had only to put them back into the sack again.

Taking hope, the girl turned next to the broken water jar. But when she saw its long crack, she started to cry again. "However much water I pour into that jar, it will never be full," she said aloud. But when she came back from the well with her first bucket, she found the crack mended with firm, hardened clay. No doubt it was a good *tokgabi* from the kitchen rafters who had taken pity on her, like the ten thousand birds. No doubt it was that *tokgabi*, too, who bewitched this first bucket so that it filled the repaired jar to the brim.

Now Nan Yang could go to the fair to hear the music, to see the acrobats, and to listen to the storytellers' fascinating tales. The wicked stepmother and two evil stepsisters were not pleased to see her there so happy and enjoying herself.

The next feast in that village was a picnic on the hillsides to view the summer scenery.

"You may go to the picnic, Dirty Pig," her unkind stepmother said to Nan Yang, "but only when you have dug out all the weeds in our rice field." The cruel woman nodded her head, satisfied that the girl could never finish that task in time. She had good reason to think so, as the rice paddy was huge and filled with weeds.

Nan Yang took up her hoe but when she struck its point into the very first clump of weeds, a huge black ox appeared close to her side. With mighty bites the animal dug all the weeds out of that field. With a dozen mouthfuls, the weeds disappeared down its throat.

"Come with me, Orchid Blossom," the huge black ox commanded. And it led the girl off to the hillside and into the woods.

When Nan Yang came at last to the picnic, her basket was filled with the ripest, the rarest, and the most delicious of fruits. All the picnickers marveled at how scrumptious the fruits were. They made much of Nan Yang, to her stepsisters' dismay.

At home that evening her stepmother demanded that Nan Yang tell them how she had managed to rid the rice field of weeds and where she found the fruit.

"We shall stay at home next time ourselves," the selfish stepsisters declared when she told them the story. "Nan Yang shall go ahead to the picnic before the black ox comes again."

When the black ox returned, it led the selfish stepsisters off into the woods. But it was not as it had been with the dutiful Nan Yang. To follow the black ox, the two selfish sisters had to crawl through tangled thickets. The twigs pulled out their hair, and the thorns tore their fine clothing. Their sullen faces were scratched. There was blood on their soft, idle hands. They made a sorry sight when they arrived at the picnic place. And there was no fruit at all in their battered baskets.

The Rabbit that Rode
on a Tortoise

AT THE SEASHORE one day, a rabbit saw a strange tortoise crawling toward him. Now all rabbits are curious, as you well know. The curious rabbit stopped hopping and wiggled its nose. It waited to see what the strange tortoise would do.

"Have you eaten your honorable food, sir?" the tortoise greeted the rabbit, just as politely as if he had been a man.

"*Yé*, I have eaten," the rabbit replied with a bow. "What brings you here?"

"I've come to explore these green hillsides," the tortoise replied. "I have heard that the view they give of the sea is very fine. I, too, wish to admire it."

"Does it please your honorable eyes?" the rabbit asked.

"I find it very dull," was the impolite answer. "It cannot compare with the views of the sea from under the water. Here on the land there are no waving plants of clear green, like the finest jade, such as there are in the undersea gardens. Here are no hills of coral, no valleys nor plains brightened by royal processions of fish with rainbow scales. You should see for yourself the many beauties and treasures of the Dragon King's watery realm."

"I should like to witness such wonders," said the rabbit, whose curiosity got the better of his judgment. "But I can't swim. How should I get there?"

"You could swim there on my back, honorable rabbit," the tortoise said persuasively, "I go so slowly that you won't fall off, and I could teach you to breathe underwater as well as on the land."

Now that tortoise spoke with honey upon his lips, but he had a knife in his heart. He meant no good to that rabbit, as you shall hear.

The best-beloved daughter of the Dragon King had been ill for many a day. No one had been able to cure her. Not the great whale, nor yet the little shrimp. Though the king had offered a rich reward, none had succeeded in finding a way to drive the evil spirits out of her body.

Then the tortoise came forward, and said, "I have heard, exalted sir, that the best cure for any ailment is the liver of a young rabbit. I know where I can find one. I think I can bring him here so that his liver may work the cure for your daughter."

The Dragon King was hopeful his daughter could be saved, so he sent the tortoise off to the seashore to bring back the rabbit. Now the tortoise is not very clever. Everyone knows that. Or why should he creep about dragging his tail in the dirt? But he was clever enough not to let the rabbit know why he was so anxious to ferry him down to the undersea palace of that Dragon King.

The rabbit miraculously became used to breathing underwater and saw spectacular sights and shining wonders as the tortoise had promised. His round eyes grew rounder at the sight of the gems and the treasures in the Dragon King's palace. He was having a great time until her heard one of the fish guards at the entrance to the Dragon King's court say, "Now that the rabbit has come, the Dragon King's daughter will surely recover. Today they'll cut his liver out. She'll gobble it up and be cured."

The dismayed rabbit gathered his wits quickly together. When they came to take out his liver, he showed no sign of fear. "Why did the tortoise not tell me it was my liver you wanted?" he said to the Dragon King, bowing politely. "Did he not know that when Hananim made us rabbits, he gave us the power to take our livers out of our bodies? When I eat too much and my liver grows hot, I remove it and cool it in the blue ocean waves. When I met the tortoise, I had just put my liver out on the beach to dry in the sun. You might have had it without so much bother, for I do not really need it myself. But now we'll have to go all the way back to get it."

The Dragon King and the tortoise believed the words of the rabbit. With his tail dragging even lower in shame, the tortoise let the rabbit climb back up onto his shell. He then ferried him across the ten thousand flashing blue waves to the safe, sunny beach.

"Where does your liver lie, honorable rabbit?" asked the tortoise, who was eager to repair his mistake.

"*Ai*, it's safe inside my body. And now I am safe too!" the rabbit rejoiced, hopping away across the sand like a young deer.

The Singing Mourner
and the Dancing Nun

ONCE THERE was a king whose greatest care and comfort were to make life better for his people.

It was the custom to dress himself as a farmer and trudge over the countryside to find out how his subjects were faring. One night he came to a poor hut echoing with the sound of singing. Curious, the King entered the gate. Softly he crept near enough to look in through a peephole in the paper window pane.

To his amazement, the King saw an old man sadly weeping, while a mourner sang and a nun danced before him. It was the young man in the mourner's garb who answered the King's knock.

"Good sir," said the King, "my lantern has gone out. May I rekindle its flame by your fire?"

"Of course, please come in," the mourner replied and helped the man relight his lantern.

"If you could indulge me for a moment," the visitor said, "could you explain these three mysteries to me? Why is it that an old man weeps, while a mourner sings and a nun dances before him?"

"Perhaps the gentleman will tell me first why he pries into the affair of another man's courts," the young mourner said, annoyed at the questions of his strange guest.

"Forgive me. It is not just idle curiosity," the King replied politely. "I ask for a purpose, young sir. If you'll enlighten me, perhaps good may come of it."

The King's words and kind manner impressed the young man. "Hunger has long lived under our roof," he explained. "Our kitchen is empty. No ant is tempted to crawl on its floor.

It's been a long time since there was enough rice even to fill our own empty stomachs. Worst of all, we have not been able to find proper food for our aged father. Each day my sister has sold a strand of her hair so that she can buy him a little bean soup. This very night her last lock was cut off. That's why she's now bald and looks like a nun."

"My father, whose mind is not so clear as once it was, thinks she has become a nun to save him from starving. For that reason he weeps. And it is to stop his weeping that I sing and she dances. I wear my mourner's robe still though my mother has been dead far longer than the appointed three years. That's because we don't have any money for new clothes."

The King's heart was touched. He looked around the poor hut, seeking a way in which to help this good son, and his eyes fell on a fine poem hanging on the wall.

"Those words are golden," he said, pointing to the wall writing. "Who wrote this?"

"They are my own poor verses, honorable gentleman," the young man said modestly. "I have some learning, but I lack money for brushes, for ink, and for paper."

"Your goodness to your father deserves a handsome reward, and such reward you shall have," the King said to the young man in the gray mourner's dress. "I can see you are well schooled. Present yourself at the Royal Examination Halls two days from now. There will be a place reserved for you." And when he departed, he left behind money for food and for buying the rabbit-hair brush, the ink paste, and some paper.

Now it was not the time of year for a King's examination. Nor had one been planned. The scholars of the capital shook their heads in amazement when it was announced that the contest would take place in two days.

They were even more puzzled at the subject that was announced. "Whoever heard of writing an essay with such a title?" they complained to one another. "An Old Man Weeps! A Mourner Sings! A Nun Dances!"

The poor young man, still in his mourner's dress, was the only one who could give meaning to such a theme. In verse, he quickly set down the story he had told his curious visitor. He was the first to throw his scroll over the fence of lances that surrounded the judges' court.

The King declared him the winner of the contest and called him to his palace. On his knees before the King, the young man bowed his head to the floor, after the custom of the Court.

"Do you not know me, excellent *paksa*?" the King asked him kindly.

"You are the King," the trembling youth managed to say. "I am also your curious visitor who came in the night," the King replied. And with his own jade fingers he placed the *paksa's* hat on the young man's head. He called for fine robes to replace the gray mourner's robe, and he hung the seal of court office on the young man's belt. He ordered a court musician to lead his triumphal march through the city. A courtier ran ahead of him bearing the beribboned scrolls that told of his great honor.

Wearing a silk coat and seated on a white horse, the son rode home in state to tell the news of his good fortune to his old father. Never again did the Spirit of Hunger fly inside their gate. Good fortune followed him and his sister. Go-betweens, offering her rich, handsome husbands, flocked to their gate. Thus was their goodness to their old father rewarded, as almost always happens.

The Ant that Laughed
Too Much

ONCE THERE was a wise old ant who was highly respected in the garden where she lived. Everyone came to her for advice, and so it wasn't strange that the earthworm should choose her to act as a go-between and find him a wife.

"I really want a good wife, Omoni," the earthworm said to the ant. "Someone who will take care of my clothes and prepare my rice and kimchi. Find me a young wife, a healthy and strong one. I know you'll choose wisely."

The ant agreed, and she was thinking over the problem one sunny afternoon, when she met a strong, healthy centipede. "How would you like to become a bride?" the ant asked the young centipede.

"Maybe. Maybe," was the centipede's reply. "But tell me about the bridegroom first."

"He's industrious. He's patient and calm," the ant replied with enthusiasm.

"Does he live in this garden?" the centipede asked.

"*Yé*, he lives in this garden, though often he is out of sight of those who walk on its paths."

"That is true of all garden creatures," the centipede said. "Tell me more about the bridegroom."

"Well, he's much longer than you are and scuttles about although he doesn't have legs."

"That's no centipede," the prospective bride said scornfully. "What would I do with a husband without any legs?"

"He is an honorable earthworm," the ant then confessed.

"*Ai*, a damp, clammy earthworm!" The centipede shook her head. "An earthworm would never work out. I'll never have the patience required to make a coat for such a long creature."

The ant thought this very funny. She laughed and she laughed as she scurried down the garden path to tell the bad news to the waiting bridegroom.

"*Ai*, Earthworm," she said between her fits of laughter. "I found a young bride, a beautiful centipede, healthy and strong, but she'll have none of you. She says she could never have a legless husband and that you're way too tall. She'd never have enough patience to sew your clothes."

"I don't find this funny," the earthworm said indignantly. "Why should a centipede laugh at a fine earthworm like me? I would not have her either. With all those legs of hers! No! Again, no! How should I ever get enough straw to make shoes for so many feet? The bargain is off."

Well, the ant thought this even funnier than the remarks of the centipede. She laughed and she laughed until her sides ached. She feared she would burst. So she took a straw rope and tied herself tightly together about her middle.

Only when she had forgotten about her adventures as go-between for the earthworm and the centipede did the ant untie the rope.

But the ant had laughed too much. Her waist was so firmly pinched in by the straw rope that it never grew large again. That's why an ant's waist is so small.

Rice from a Cat's Fur

A SCHOLAR named Yo had become so wise that his fame spread across the land, eventually reaching the ears of the King himself.

"Send for that Scholar Yo," the King commanded. "He's sure to give us the best advice and counsel. I'll give him a job in my court, and he'll wear a precious peacock feather in his hat."

Yo seemed to become increasingly poor. While the other ministers grew rich in their offices, Yo seemed to grow poor. He was so busy in his court position that he gave no thought to his own affairs. His three daughters, who looked after his house, often found no rice in the storeroom. Their father had thoughtlessly given it all to the beggars who came to his gate.

On top of it, Yo was being sent on a special mission to China. Who better than this wise minister, sent on a Dragon Throne, to help the emperor? But it was an incredibly long journey. It would take three years for Yo to complete his task.

"*Ai-go! Ai-go!* What shall we do?" Yo's daughters wept when their father announced his departure. "We have but one dress apiece, *Abuji*. Two of us must wash the dress of the other. She must remain hidden under the coverlids until we have brought it out from under the ironing sticks. And there's only one jar of rice left in our storeroom. What will we eat when you're gone and we've run out of money?"

In this household, the master's favorite pet was a clever, black cat. When Yo bent over his books in his Hall of Perfect Learning, the cat lay in his lap. It purred and it purred while the man rubbed the soft fur just under its chin. One strange thing about this cat was that it never closed its eyes. No one had ever caught it asleep. It just lay still, purred and purred, and watched over the household.

"Of course you will eat, my daughters," Yo said, as he climbed into his traveling chair. "Heaven will care for you while I am gone. If you run out of rice and there's no other food left, turn to my black cat. Rub his fur carefully like this." The man ran his slim fingers through the soft fur of the cat, which had jumped into his lap. He began at its tail, and he stroked its fur towards its head. Then he gently handed the black cat down into the arms of one of his daughters.

But the girls didn't love the black cat as much as their father did, and they soon forgot his parting words. As long as the rice in their storeroom held out, they managed to get by. But they ate only nine times in a month and were always hungry. Eventually the last storage jar grew empty and there was not a single grain of rice left in the household.

"We have to sell our belongings," the sisters cried. Fine chests bound with brass, handsome embroidered silks, even their treasured hairpins of silver and coral had to be sold to give them money for rice. But that too was quickly eaten up. Soon their house was as empty as the rice jars in the storeroom.

"What was it our father said about the black cat?" one sister then asked the others.

"Perhaps he spoke a riddle which will help us get food," another sister suggested.

"If only we could remember what he said about the black cat!" the third one cried.

That evening, as they sat hungry in their inner chamber, the black cat jumped into the lap of the youngest girl. "Now I remember, this is how you rub his fur," she cried, and she began to run her fingers gently along the cat's soft furry back from his tail to his head. It did the trick.

"Hé! Hai! Hai!" they all cried. "Rice is pouring out of the cat's fur!"

It was true! Before their very eyes a steady stream of rice grains fell out of the fur of their father's black cat. Fine, whole grains they were, white as the snow of winter, clean and smooth enough for the cooking pot. The more the girl rubbed the cat's fur, the more rice showered from it. It made a huge mound on the clean floor.

That evening, Yo's house was filled with laughter and rejoicing. Once more his daughters' stomachs were full, and the days ahead seemed as rosy and fair as the rising sun. Never would they be hungry again, no matter how long their father was away.

The sisters took turns in rubbing the black cat's soft fur. When they had more rice than they needed to fill their jars, they sold the surplus. Now they could buy back their fine brassbound chests, their handsome embroideries, and their precious hairpins of coral and silver. Now they could buy cloth for new dresses, and even black oil to make their hair neat and shining.

At the end of three years Yo returned from the court of the Chinese emperor with his mission accomplished. As soon as he had greeted his daughters, he called for his black cat. When he heard how the magic rice had flowed from its fur to save them from starvation, he declared, "Now I am home again. I have secured for the King the aid our land needs from China. My reward will be great. Our coffers will overflow, and our food jars will never again be empty. Most of all, we'll never have to rub rice out of my cat's fur again."

He was right. Secretly the youngest girl tried rubbing the cat's fur from its tail to its head. But the cat only purred and purred and watched over the household through his wide-open eyes.

The Beggars' Friend

A SPOONMAKER named Woo lived in a modest house on the Street of Spoonmakers. Woo was a kind husband and a good father. There were always bundles of grass for mending holes in his roof. There was always fresh rice straw to make sandals for his children's feet. And there were always rice and kimchi in the brown jars in his court.

Woo had a heart as big as the sky. When his children were small and needed clothing and food, he took care of them first. But when his son was grown up and his daughters were married, he began to give more and more to the beggars who knocked at the gate of his spoonmaking shop. It was a bowl of rice to this one and a few coins for that one. Of course a few coins won't buy a coat or a pig, but if you put enough raindrops together you'll have a river. And like a river, money flowed out of Woo's money chests into the outstretched hands of these hungry beggars.

How those fellows fought to get to their friend, Woo the Spoonmaker! The minute he appeared at his gate, the beggars came running. Night after night, he returned home without a single coin in the money belt his wife had made for him.

Eventually, there was nothing left in the money chests, nothing to buy food with and no more brass to forge the shining spoons that earned their keep. As is often the case, Woo began to borrow money. When he couldn't pay his debts, he was hauled before a judge.

It was only when the jailers found out Woo had nothing to give them that they let him go. The bruised and beaten Woo, that sad and sorry spoonmaker, made his way home, limping through the muddy streets.

Woo was just entering his gate when when he stubbed his toe on something hard. Looking down in the dirt to see what it could be, he found seven coins tied in a straw string.

"Not a lot of money," Woo said to his wife, "but it will at least buy some rice for our dinner." He sent his son out to buy the provisions.

Woo had removed five coins to give to his son. Yet when he looked down at the string bundle, it still contained seven coins. He could not believe his eyes. He called his good wife to come and count the coins also. He pulled off four more coins; still seven remained. When Woo lay down on the floor to sleep that night, the riddle still puzzled him. He rose again and again to test the cash string. No matter how many times he pulled coins off of its end, always seven were left.

"Thus is goodness rewarded," his wife said to Woo. And they hid their magic coin bundle and didn't breathe a word of it to anyone.

Once again, bright shining spoons were being made in Woo's house on the Street of the Spoonmakers. So if the neighbors wondered about the new roof on his house and the fine new hat the man wore, they could think they were bought with money his customers paid him.

Woo's heart remained as big as the sky, and he still gave to the poor. But he made his gifts in secret now so the judge and jailers wouldn't drag him back to the prison. Instead of strewing money about through the crowds on the streets, he made journeys into the country, tossing coins over the gates of the poorer households. Or he went even farther into the hills to the temple of the Great Buddha. There he gave handfuls of coins to the priests for their poor boxes.

At the same time there were puzzled faces in the Royal Treasure House. "Why is so much money disappearing?" the king's treasurer asked his assistants.

They shook their heads. They each knew how many coins they had secretly slipped into their own pockets, but that didn't account for all the missing money. So who was the thief? The assistants stood guard while the King's Treasurer watched.

One morning at daybreak the Treasurer heard a sharp, clinking sound on the tops of the cash piles. To his amazement, several coins rose into the air and flew out through a hole in the Treasury roof. Off they went, by twos and by threes, by fours and by fives. Each time Woo pulled coins out of his magic bundle, coins were whisked away. By closely watching, the Treasurer could see them riding the wind to the roof of Woo's little house.

The good *tokgabi* who had left the magic bundle at Woo's gate gave the spoonmaker warning before the Treasury guards came to get him.

"Take our magic bundle and hide it," Woo said to his wife. "Then make your way to the temple of the Great Buddha. The good priests will give us shelter. Wait there till I arrive!"

With their son his wife set out at once for the faraway temple on the Diamond Mountain. The magic bundle was safely tucked away, far inside her sleeve.

The Treasury guards came, and Woo was again brought before the Judge. But this time, he wasn't punished. A man who knew such secrets was far too valuable. "Perhaps," the judge thought, "this spoonmaker can be persuaded to send money through the air and into my pocket too."

Now Woo had no intention of parting with the secret of his magic bundle of coins. He hatched a plan to secure his freedom and avoid being returned to jail.

"Honorable Judge," this spoonmaker said craftily, "I will indeed show you the secret of my coins that ride on the wind. But it will take time. I need a large sheet of paper, some ink and an inkstone, and a rabbit-hair pen."

The paper was pasted onto a broad screen where Woo began drawing black lines with the pen. The attendants gaped as they saw appear, there before their very eyes, a life-sized donkey. The little round eyes, the stiff hairy mane, the tiny neat hoofs, the long tufted tail, one after another, each part of the donkey's body came into being under Woo's brush.

"I mustn't work too fast. My wife needs time to escape," Woo thought to himself, and he took great pains in drawing the nose and the mouth of the donkey. The courtiers began to laugh and to whisper, "It looks just like the Judge."

"But it has only one ear," one onlooker said.

"That's like the Judge, too. He never hears but one side of a case," another declared. And they fell to laughing louder and louder.

Hearing them, the judge came to look at the donkey too. He flew into a rage, for he too saw the likeness. "Throw this man in jail," cried the angry official. But Woo quickly brushed in the other ear, and the picture was finished.

At once the paper donkey began to move its head. With a loud heehaw a live animal trotted right out of the screen. Woo leaped on its back, and the donkey galloped away. Across the courtyard and out of the open gate it went before the astonished guards could stop it. And that was the last those people ever saw of Woo, the beggars' friend.

He eventually caught up with his wife. Though the people of Seoul never saw him again, they still heard of his kindness. The beggars followed him to his new home in the Temple of the

Great Buddha on the Diamond Mountain. And they received from the priests there alms which Woo provided. So long as Woo lived, cash from the Royal Treasure House still rode on the winds to refill his magic bundle.

The Village of the Pure Queen

THEY say that she was called Kang and that she was only a simple girl who lived far out in the country. One evening when Kang was drawing water up from the village well, a general rode up on horseback. He was an important man, as one could see by the number of servants who ran by his side and by the number of soldiers who served as his bodyguards.

The day was scorching, and the journey had been long. The General's face was the color of a red peony bloom. Beads of water made tiny brooks that trickled down his broad cheeks. "Give me water to drink," the General said to the girl, after they had exchanged polite greetings.

Kang bowed, filling a big bowl with water freshly drawn from the well. But before she handed the bowl up to the great man, she plucked a number of tender green willow leaves and dropped them into the cold water.

The General took the bowl in his hands and began to drink.

He was greatly annoyed when he found how the willow leaves got in his way. Instead of taking huge gulps, which his thirst called for, he was forced to sip slowly.

When he had drained the bowl of its contents, he gently scolded the girl.

"It wasn't very polite to throw leaves into my drinking bowl," the General said to Kang.

"It was only because I feared for the health of the Great General," the young girl replied. "You were overheated and tired, honorable sir. If you gulped down the water too quickly, you'd have swallowed the spirits of sickness along with it. You might even have died. It was to prevent this that I put the willow leaves into the bowl. They forced you to drink slowly with very small sips. Thus no harm could come to you."

The General said to himself, "This young woman is as wise as she is beautiful. There is love for her in my heart." So he turned to Kang and declared, "I will make you my bride if you will but wait until the war ends."

So she waited and waited, and at last the war was over. When Kang's bridegroom came riding on his white horse, who should he be but this very same General. And who should that general have been but the famous General Yi, who later became King of our Dragon Backed Country.

This king had many other wives living in his palace, but Queen Kang was the one he admired most. Her wisdom shed light on his most difficult problems of state, and he always consulted her.

No doubt she even had a voice in choosing the location of this city of Seoul. Her sedan chair was carried just behind the chair of the King when the valley in the mountains was selected for his new capital, and she had a voice in choosing her own grave site.

"When I have mounted the Dragon, you must build a huge kite and write my name *Kang* upon it," the good Queen said to the King. "Let the wind take the kite high into the air above the

Royal Palace. Then break the string and where the kite falls, let my spirit rest there."

The King complied, sending the enormous kite up into the sky. With his own jade fingers, he cut its string. Like a great wounded butterfly, the kite slowly fluttered down to the earth. On the little ridge where it landed, Queen Kang's tomb was built.

Called the Pure Tomb, it remained there for many years, close to the Palace. The sad King liked to listen to the music of the bells in the little temple above it. He thought they were like the soft voice of his departed Queen Kang.

A Story for Sale

YI was a rich fellow who lived with his wife far out in the country and far up on a hillside. Their brass-bound chests overflowed, and they hid part of their wealth in in huge kimchi jars buried deep in their courtyard.

There were no sons in that house far up on the hillside, and no grandchildren to bother. It was as still as the ancestors' tomb under Yi's roof. The old couple often were lonely. Traveling actors or storytellers never knocked at their gate, so far off the road. They were too old to go in their sedan chairs to pay visits or find amusement at the town fairs. Today was like tomorrow, and the evenings were long.

One morning the master of the house said to Hap, his gate-keeper, "Go down to the valley and don't stop walking until you've found a good storyteller. Buy from him a fine tale. You can pay him one hundred coins for it!"

Hap wasn't particularly bright. He wouldn't have known a storyteller from a woodcutter. But he loaded the chest containing the cash on a wooden carrying frame called a jiggy and placed it on his back. Then he trotted off down the hillside in search of a fine tale to bring back to his master.

Hap walked many hours along the path through the valley before he met anyone. Then he came on a farmer, resting by the side of a stream that ran through some rice fields.

"Have you been in peace, venerable sir?" Hap said, bowing in polite greeting.

"*Yé*, Uncle, and you, have you eaten your honorable meals?" the stranger returned his courtesy, according to custom.

"Will the Learned Man tell me if he has a story which he will sell? My Master has ordered me to buy a fine tale."

Now this stranger was a farmer, not a storyteller. He certainly didn't have a story on the tip of his tongue, nor could he remember one. But he needed the money and didn't want to let such a good chance slip by.

"*Yé*, Uncle, I have a story," he said to the gatekeeper. "But it will cost a large sum. How much can your Master pay?"

"How about a hundred coins? That is all I have in this money box."

The farmer was thrilled when he heard Hap's offer, and he nodded his head. He thought for a moment, as he still couldn't recall a ripping good yarn and didn't have the wits to invent one. As he looked about, desperate for a story to pop into his head, he saw a long-legged stork, picking its way through the rice field. Daintily lifting first one leg and then the other, the great bird moved towards the stream.

"He's coming nearer, step by step," said the farmer. The gatekeeper, thinking the man was beginning the story, repeated his words. He must know this fine tale by heart so that he could tell it to the Master.

"He comes! Step by step!" Hap echoed. "Step by step he comes nearer!"

At that moment the stork saw a movement in the rice, and he halted to find out just what it was. "Now he stops to listen! Now he stops to look!" the farmer said with his eyes still on the stork.

"Now he stops to listen! Now he stops to look!" the gate-keeper chanted.

The rice plants no longer moved, and the stork bent his neck to hunt for some good morsel, an earthworm or perhaps a snail on the ground. With bent legs and slow steps the bird crept through the field.

"He bends down! He creeps!" the farmer went on, hoping that the stork would furnish him with a satisfactory tale. And the gatekeeper spoke likewise, reciting each word with great care.

Then there was a quick movement in the rice, and a fox raised its black nose out of the green. With a leap off the ground the stork spread its broad wings and flew quickly to safety.

"*Ai! Ai!*" cried the farmer. "He's off! He is fleeing. Soon he will be safe!"

"He's off. He is fleeing. Soon he will be safe!" his listener cried too.

"Is that all the story?" Hap asked the stranger when no more words came from his lips.

"Yeah, that's all. Who could want more?" the farmer said haughtily, and he loaded Hap's bag of coins onto the jiggy.

On his way home up the hillside, Hap repeated the story over and over, proud that he hadn't forgotten a single word. Of course he did not understand it, but then he was a dark, unlearned fellow.

When Hap recited the tale, Old Yi and his wife found it be an odd story. Like the gatekeeper, they didn't understand it. The old man recited it over and over at night, trying to puzzle out its meaning.

One evening, in that remote and lonely region, a wicked man came to rob the prosperous old couple. The robber was young, and it was no trouble for him to climb over the wall. With soft steps the thief was making his way toward the house, when he heard a voice say, "He comes! Step by step! Step by step he comes nearer."

This brought the thief to a standstill. "The man can't possibly see me, so how can he know I'm here?" he thought to himself. He held his breath, listening and looking about him.

Then the voice came again. "Now he stops to listen! Now he stops to look!"

The thief couldn't understand how the man inside the house knew just what he was doing. But he was bold, and he began to creep toward the light shining through the window paper.

"He bends down! He creeps!" The voice of Yi, telling the story to his old wife, came clearer and clearer.

"How can he know each thing I do?" the robber thought. He began to be frightened. "This must be the house of a spirit," he said to himself. "I had best get out of here."

And as he turned to run away, the voice of Old Yi followed him. "He's off," it cried. "Soon he will be safe!"

The thief ran as fast as ever he could, leaping the wall at the very first try and never stopping until he reached his gang of thieves in the town down in the valley.

All those wicked men shook their heads at the tale their frightened friend told them. And none of them ever again tried to rob the house of Old Yi who bought the farmer's story for a hundred coins!"

The Two Stone Giants

THERE once was a rich man named Yong who lived in an imposing mansion with five different gates. Along with his immense wealth, Yong had a kind heart. Like Woo the Spoonmaker, he never could bring himself to turn beggars away from his gate.

So the beggars flocked to his door. Buddhist priests with their begging bowls and little brass bells; poor farmers whose rice plants had yielded no grain that year; even city folk who'd been swindled by shysters, they all traveled the well-worn path to Yong's open gates. The household servants ran back and forth from morning until night putting rice and money into the outstretched hands of the beggars.

But when water is always poured out of a bowl and none is poured in, the bowl soon is empty, my little dragons. So it was with Yong's cash chests. He became frightened at the lessening number of the coins on their bottoms.

One afternoon a traveler knocked at the gate and asked if he might come in for a rest. This one was an old man, and he wore a poet's hat. Yong invited the aged scholar into his House of Guests. He offered him a bowl of hot rice and a cup of good wine to refresh him.

"Wisdom drips from your tongue, honorable sir," Yong said to his visitor. "Give me some advice. I've given away so much food and money to the beggars who crowd my gate that soon my entire fortune will be gone. Yet I can't bring myself to turn them away. What can I do?"

The old man sat quietly thinking before offering his suggestion. "It's very simple. If the Great Man will come out with me into the courtyard, I will show him the way." There he pointed to two tall pillars of stone which jutted out of a cliff not far away. "Make those two rocks into *miryeks*. Carve them into a giant man and a giant woman. When the great stone figures are completed, I promise you no more beggars will come to your gate." When the old man had departed, Yong considered the man's counsel. "Making *miryeks* would cost too much," he said at first. But so many more beggars clamored for cash that he decided to follow the old man's advice.

The stone carvings were expensive to create, costing all the cash in the man's coffers. But finally the two giant *miryeks* stood there, as tall and as powerful as they look today. Each wore a stone hat on its head and stone robes on its shoulders.

Not long thereafter the learned old traveler again called at Yong's gate. But Yong had no pleasant, polite words of welcome for him this time. He grabbed him by his gray topknot, and he shook him well. "How dare you come back here again, Old Man?" he cried. "You have brought ruin upon me, you and your *miryeks*!"

But the old man only smiled and asked, "Will the Great Man be pleased to have a little patience? What was the charm you asked of me?"

"I asked for a charm to keep beggars away."

"And didn't the charm work? I don't see any beggars at your gate."

Yong looked crestfallen. "No, there are no beggars there," he admitted, "because they know I have nothing left to give."

"Then you shouldn't complain. I gave you what you asked for, and you've learned what everyone else in this land knows—the only place where beggars are not is where there is nothing to be given away."

Yong bowed to the old man, begging his pardon. "You're again right in your wisdom. I'm the one who's been foolish. But it would've been better for me to empty my coffers for poor and hungry beggars rather than for those two people of stone."

The Mole and the Miryek

ALL fathers and mothers think their children are perfect. Even the porcupine says its little ones are pleasant and smooth to the touch. So it was with a mother Mole. Deep in her underground home, she believed her daughter to be the perfect child. Her skin was like softest satin, and her little nose and her claws were delicately pointed. Truly she was a perfect mole.

"Where will we find a husband good enough for our dear daughter?" the mole asked his wife. She deserves the ideal mate to match her perfection."

"We could send the go-between to the King of the Moles," the mother replied. The mother replied. "Nowhere in his kingdom would he find a bride so fair as our beautiful daughter."

"I think we can do better than the King of the Moles," the father countered. "Only the very best will do for my little princess. The sky looks down on the mole King. So I'll go to the sky."

"But I'm not the almighty," the sky said when the mole came

to his gate. "The sun rules over me. The sun tells me when I am to be bright and when I am to be dark. Go find the sun, if you seek the most powerful presence in the universe."

"That's not me either," said the sun to the Mole. "It's the cloud that tells me when my face is to be bright and when it's to be darkened. Go find the cloud."

So the mole knocked at the gate of the Cloud King. There he received this reply. "It is true I cover the sun. I send forth the lightning. In my hands I hold the thunder. But I'm not the almighty. Go find the wind. It blows and blusters, scattering us clouds across the sky."

When the mole stood before the wind, he trembled. Now he was sure he'd found the most powerful presence in the universe. "I seek the one who has power over all things," he said, bowing low to the wind. "My daughter is so perfect that he's the only one good enough to be her husband."

"I'm not the most powerful, honorable Mole," the wind said, blowing forth his great puffing breath. "It's true I send the clouds and the rain wherever I want. I can snap trees in half. But there's one thing over which I have no power. That is the stone *miryek* that stands just above your underground home. I can puff and I can blow, but I cannot move that stone man even the breadth of a fly's wing."

The revelation came as a surprise to the ambitious Mole. So he went back home again and bowed before the stone giant that towered so high above his underground home.

"*Yé*, honorable neighbor," the *miryek* said when the mole had told him of his quest, "it's true that I'm strong. The sky can't harm me, and the sun can't melt me, no matter how fiercely it burns. The clouds, with their rain, their lightning and thunder, will never topple me. In the entire universe, I only fear one person."

"Tell me who it is, great *miryek*," begged the the creature. "It is a mole."

"A mole? How could that be, great one? A mole is but a small creature, living deep in the ground."

"But it is only a mole who can dig the earth from under my feet. Should a mole dig there long enough, I would begin to topple over. Should he keep on digging, in time I would be lying face down on the earth. So the mole is the only thing I fear."

Now at last the mole was satisfied that he had discovered the husband best suited for his daughter. He called in the go-between, and they soon arranged a marriage with a fine, handsome young mole. The couple raised a brood of babies in their cozy underground home and lived happily ever after.

The King's Seventh Daughter

THERE once was a King who had six daughters. He loved his girls but also wanted to be blessed with a son. The fringe of straw announcing a baby's birth had been hung across the palace gate six times. Not once had there been bits of charcoal knotted in it to indicate the birth of a son.

"Don't worry," the courtiers advised the King. "Next time you'll surely have a boy." But the seventh child was also a girl. The King was so disappointed that he issued a shocking proclamation. "I won't have another daughter. Throw her into the sea!"

The Queen wept bitter tears. She loved her daughters but had to obey's her husband's royal orders. So the baby girl was locked inside a stone chest which was taken by boat far out to sea. There it was dropped into the deep, deep, deep water. But instead of sinking, the heavy chest rode the flashing blue waves like a stone boat. At last it washed up onshore at the feet of a good priest. "Here's the royal seal," the priest said. "This chest surely contains a prize of great value." Carefully opening the stone box, he found inside a beautiful baby girl, smiling brightly as if she had been in her dear mother's arms.

Well, this priest knew the story of the King's Seventh Daughter. He feared that her angry father might harm the poor child if he found out that she'd been spared. So he hid her in the temple. He fed her and clothed her and made her days happy.

"Who am I, Holy One?" the princess asked her protector when she was old enough to wonder about her mother and father.

"You are a daughter of the forest, my little one," the kind priest replied. "Your father was the Spirit of the Bamboo, and your mother dwelt in the Odong Tree." So the girl always made her bows to the bamboo and the odong, just as though they were human.

As the years went by, the King's seventh daughter grew up safe and sound there in the temple. She never learned the truth of her royal birth until one day a *mudang* came looking for the priest.

"The Queen has fallen ill," the *mudang* said. "She's failing fast and will die unless her lost daughter is found. I believe you can help me bring her to the Queen's chamber."

"The King will be irate that his orders to kill his youngest daughter were not followed. She's in great danger," the good priest objected.

"Neither the girl nor her protector need have any fears," the *mudang* declared, "it's the King himself who seeks his lost daughter to save his wife's life."

Everyone rejoiced when the King's seventh daughter appeared at the court. While the Queen didn't die, she didn't entirely recover either.

"There's a certain medicine in faraway India," the *mudang* said to the King. "Only one of the Queen's daughters can get it for her, and only when that's been accomplished will the evil spirits depart at last from her royal body."

Now India lies far beyond the broad plains and the high mountains of China. There were ten thousand chances against a traveler's safely going there and safely returning. The six older daughters all flatly refused to attempt the perilous journey. But the good seventh daughter, who had been reared by the priest, consented to go.

Over the broad plains, across the deep rivers, and beyond the high mountains she traveled to seek the much-needed medicine for her mother. Then over the high mountains, across the deep rivers, and across the broad plains she journeyed back again. Two long years it took her, but at last the medicine was brought and the good Queen was cured.

"What an incredibly wise *mudang*," the courtiers cried "If she hadn't found the King's seventh daughter for us, our Queen would have died."

"The King's youngest daughter is amazing!" the *mudangs* proclaimed. "If she hadn't undertaken that long and dangerous journey to bring back the medicine, our cure wouldn't have worked." That is why the *mudangs* made the King's seventh daughter their own guardian spirit. Even today, they call on her name in their songs that drive out the demons.

It's also why—as a tribute to the devotion and kindness of a loyal daughter—when you mourn a father who's passed, you always carry a bamboo staff. If it's your mother who has ridden the dragon to the Distant Shore, the staff is made of odong wood.

The Woodcutter and the
Old Men of the Mountain

MIN the woodcutter lived in the days before the trees on the mountainsides were all cut down. It would have been a pleasantly perfect life under the grass roof of Min's little house, if his wife didn't have such a disagreeable disposition. She scolded him all day long.

Who can blame the woodcutter for wanting to get away from his temperamental wife? He often sang as he trudged up the wooded mountainside. His jiggy was a far lighter load on his back than the smacks and blows his wife gave him with her ironing sticks.

As Min walked along, he composed a poem about the pleasures of a solitary walk in the country. Soon he turned the words into a song:

> "Ho, the strong jiggy
> Rests light on my back.

Of branches and twigs,
For my stove there's no lack."

"I'll pile them on high,
Then pile on some more,
Until I've enough
To silence her roar."

It was as quiet and peaceful on the mountainside as within a temple. Because the sun was to bright and the sky so blue, Min climbed higher and higher. He stopped now and then to bathe his face in the crystal water of a stream or to admire the wildflowers that grew amid the rocks.

Then he came upon a little clearing hidden among the trees, just the place for him to rest after his climb. But a group of curiously dressed old men were seated there in the shade of a tree. They were playing a game of changki on a flat stone between them.

With a polite cough of warning Min drew near the players. The old men looked up from their game to greet him.

"Our visitor looks tired. No doubt he is thirsty," the oldest one said. "Give him a bowl of *sool*, boy," he commanded the young servant who squatted nearby. Min sat down beside the Ancient Ones, drinking the wine and watching their game.

The Ancient Ones played slowly. They studied each move, and their wrinkled old hands crept back and forth over their chessmen, like snails on the ground. In the soft warm air Min grew drowsy. As he watched the game, his head nodded. Soon he was asleep, his head lifting with a jerk when a player cried, "*Chang*," as he made a checkmate.

At last Min opened his eyes to see that the sun was low in the sky. "My wife will be irate if I stay much longer," he said to himself, about to stand up. What could have happened to him? His joints were aching and stiff. He could scarcely get onto his feet. And when he looked down at his clothes, he found they were ragged and tattered. What was this white hair that fell from his chin? His beard and his hair were as snowy as those of the four ancient *changki* players. And where were they now? They'd disappeared without a trace.

"Those Ancient Ones must've been Mountain Spirits," Min cried aloud. "They've put a spell on me. They've taken away my good clothes and left me only these rags. They've stolen my ax. In its place they have put this crumbling stick of old wood and this rusty bit of iron. Even my jiggy frame has turned into dust, eaten up by worms. *Ai-go! Ai-go!*" Min wailed. "What will my wife say?"

With tottering steps the poor woodcutter made his way down the mountain. As he drew near his village, the world around him seemed just as strange.

"The village didn't look like this when I went up the hillside this morning," he said to himself. "There wasn't a house here on the edge of the rice fields. My oldest friend Cho didn't have green grass growing on his roof. And who are all these new people gathered about the foodseller's shop?"

There was even a strange dog in Min's own courtyard. "Whom are you looking for?" asked a young passerby, trying not to notice the woodcutter's tattered rags.

"I'm looking for Min's house, the woodcutter. Isn't this it?"

"This was Min's house," the man replied, "but he's been dead for over thirty years. His son lives here now, but he is out on the rice fields."

"And where is Min, the woodcutter?" the poor fellow asked.

"That's the sad part, Grandfather," the man replied. "It happened long before I was born, but they say he went out on the mountain to get brushwood, and he never came back. Perhaps a tiger ate him up. Or perhaps the spirits carried him off for cutting wood from a grave site."

"But I am Min the woodcutter, and this is my house," the old man declared to the crowd that had gathered. The people looked at one another in amazement and fright.

"How can a man return from the dead? Can he rise out of his grave to live again?" they cried. They cursed Min, shaking their fists in his face and then running away.

Tears rolled down the wrinkled cheeks of the old woodcutter, for he was old, as old as the men of the mountain who had played *changki* under the tree in the glen. Just then there came toward the gate a very old woman whose hair was also white. Her face had ten thousand wrinkles, and she carried a pair of ironing sticks in her hand.

"Can you tell me where I can find the wife of Min, the woodcutter?" the bewildered man asked politely. He was afraid to identify himself as Min again. This old woman might mistake him for a demon and curse him as well. But she only stared at him for a moment. Then she began to berate him. "I know you well, Old Man, even after these thirty years. You're Min himself, and I'm your wife. How could you leave me all this time to work my hands to the bone to feed our young son? You worthless man, I'll teach you to go away like that again." She seized the old man by his white topknot and began to smack his shoulders with her ironing sticks.

Dodging her blows, Min declared, "This is the best homecoming ever. At last I've returned. At least my wife hasn't changed a bit. And she hasn't forgotten me!"

The Good Brother's Reward

ONCE long ago there were two brothers, a rich one named Sang Chip and one named Sang Hun who had fallen into the hands of misfortune. When their father died, the oldest son took all the family wealth for himself. Instead of filling his father's place as head of the house and looking after his younger brother, he put him out of the gate to seek shelter and food and clothes for his family wherever he might.

In the lavish family compound, Sang Chip lived alone with only his wife. No children had been sent to bless his selfish days. Sang Hun, on the other hand, lived with his wife and several sons in a little mud hut. Its ancient grass roof had so many holes in it that the rain dripped down onto his family's heads. At night they slept on their tattered straw mats on a cold earthen floor. It was only by lying, huddled together, that they could keep warm.

By weaving straw shoes and by doing whatever jobs he could find, Sang Hun barely managed to keep his little family alive. His children often complained of hunger. Even the rats complained to their neighbors that there was not one grain of rice in that house for the stealing.

"Send our youngest son to ask help from your rich brother," Sang Hun's wife said one day to her unhappy husband. "Surely when he sees that small boy's hungry look, he will give us a little from his great store of food."

But the greedy brother turned the boy away from his gate. "I have enough food only for my own household," he said roughly. "My rice and my bean flour both are locked up tight in the storehouse. My bran I need for my cows. What extra grain there might be must go to my chickens. If I give you scraps from our table, my dogs will be angry. Now get out of here, before they attack you!"

When the little boy returned home, he was ashamed to repeat the cruel words his uncle had spoken. He only said, "I've returned empty handed as our uncle wasn't home."

"So I'll sell these shoes I'm wearing," his mother said. "Their straw soles are still good. They'll bring enough cash for a little rice for our supper."

But that night luck found its way to the good brother again. Sang Hun brought a treasure, ginseng root, back from his day of gathering wood out on the mountainside. Even the King and Queen put ginseng in their spring soups. The medicine sellers paid Sang Hun a large sum for the ginseng. His wife's shoes could now be bought back. Along with her husband, she could once again go out looking for work.

Sang Hun's wife found a place among women winnowing rice, and the man acted as a porter with his wooden jiggy frame on his back, carrying loads for the rich folk of the village. And so they got through the winter.

Spring came, and the swallows flew back from the south to build their nests under the straw eaves of Sang Hun's little house. Soon there were baby birds in those nests. One day while Sang Hun was weaving sandals out in his courtyard, he saw a long

snake glide out from the straw eaves towards the little birds.
Before the man could drive the snake away, it had gobbled up
all but one of the young swallows. That one had fallen out of
the nest and struck the hard ground. When the man picked it
up, he saw that one of its legs was broken.

Gently, bighearted Sang Hun bound up the swallow's leg
with splints made of dried fish skin. The children fed the bird
and nursed it until it could hop about once again. Its leg healed
slightly crooked, but the bird was strong enough to fly about,
chirping with joy.

When the days began to grow short and the autumn nights
began to grow chill, the little bird with the crooked leg hopped
once more across Sang Hun's courtyard. It was chirping and
chirping as if saying goodbye before it flew off to the south.

The next Spring the swallow with the crooked leg returned.
It landed on Sang Hun's hand, dropping a curious seed into
his palm. On one side of the seed the man's name was written
in golden brush strokes. On the other side were the words
Water me!

The seed had been sent by the King of the Birds as a reward
for Sang Hun's kindness in saving the baby swallow from the
snake and for healing its broken leg.

Well, that seed sprouted and grew. Its plant climbed high up
to the grass roof of that little house, and three enormous gourds
hung from its thick vine. About the middle of the Ninth Moon
the man said to his wife, "We shall cut the gourds down today.
We can eat their soft pulp and we can make water bowls out of
their hard shells."

When Sang Hun split the first gourd open, the couple came
upon a strange sight. Two servants stepped out carrying a fine
table. They carried a fine table laden with silver bowls and bottles of wine. "This bottle contains wine that gives men long
life," the spirit servants said to Sang Hun. "This bottle has wine
which makes the blind see. And this one will bring back speech
to a muted man."

The man and his family were speechless, filled with wonder as they split open the second gourd. At once their courtyard was filled with shining chests, with rich silks and rolls of shining grass linen. When the third gourd was opened, an army of carpenters appeared with tools and long, strong boards. Before the bewildered man's eyes, houses with tiled roofs, stables for horses, and storehouses and for grain rose. A long train of bullocks, loaded with furniture and jars of rice, streamed through the gate. Servants, horses, everything a wealthy household required came to Sang Hun out of these three magic gourds.

Now news travels fast, and it was not long before Sang Hun's older brother heard of his good fortune. The greedy man came hurrying to find out how it had happened. When good Sang Hun told him the story of the swallow with the crooked leg, Sang Chip determined to try the same magic himself.

With his cane he struck at every little bird he met during his journey home. Many he killed, but at last one little sparrow's leg was broken so the cruel man caught it easily. He bound up the sparrow's leg with dried fish-skin splints. He kept it inside his house until the bird could hop again, just as Sang Hun had done. But there was no kindness in Sang Chip's cruel actions, and there was no twittering of thanks when that sparrow flew away from his courts. Instead, it loudly twittered when telling the King of the Birds about cruel Sang Chip who had broken its leg.

When the sparrow with the crooked leg came back in the spring, it brought a seed for this brother, too. Greedy Sang Chip watched with delight when the green vine from it began to climb the side of his house. But the plant grew far too fast. It grew and it grew, until it smothered his entire dwelling. Its great creeping vines pried loose his roof tiles. Rain poured in upon all his treasured possessions. It cost him a fortune to have his roof entirely replaced.

Instead of three gourds there were twelve on his plant, giant balls almost as big as a huge kimchi jar. When the Ninth Moon came around, Sang Chip hired a carpenter to split open the gourds.

Out of the first gourd stepped a troupe of traveling rope dancers. It cost Sang Chip another small fortune before those traveling dancers would go away from his courts. Even more money was needed to get rid of the procession of priests who came out of the second gourd. They demanded ten thousand coins for rebuilding their temple of Buddha.

Each gourd, sawed in two, brought fresh demands on Sang Chip's cash chests. A funeral procession, whose mourners had to be paid! A band of *gesang*, those singing girls whose music and dancing and bright waving flags always cost so much! Traveling acrobats! A clown who needed funds for a long journey! A horde of officials demanding their cut of his tax money! And a band of *mudang* women, who threatened to bring the spirits of sickness into the house instead of driving them out! All these pests came out of the gourds to take away this greedy man's money. Jugglers, blind fortunetellers, and poets had to be paid, until little was left. From the eleventh gourd a giant emerged, leaving with Sang Chip's very last copper coin.

"At least we have the twelfth gourd," Sang Chip's weeping wife cried. "Surely we have been punished enough. Surely there will be food or something else good inside this last one." But when the carpenter sawed the twelfth gourd in two, clouds of smoke and hot darting flames sputtered out, destroying every house, stable and storeroom within the affluent brother's walls. His money gone, now his property had been destroyed.

With his house burned to the ground, where could this selfish man seek shelter?

"We need to ask my brother for help," he said to his wife.

"But won't he turn us away from his gates, as you turned away his hungry child?" the woman asked.

"I don't think so," Sang Chip replied. "Sang Hun has a heart as wide as the sky. He follows the ways of our father, who was always overly generous."

Sang Chip was right. His good younger brother opened gates to them and brought out tables filled with food. He also made a place for his greedy older brother, for there was plenty of room in the huge houses the King of the Birds had rewarded him with.

The Pansu and the Stableboy

SIN, the stableboy, was sent on an important journey to a distant town. He carried a present to his master's friend, who was soon to celebrate his sixty-first birthday there. The young man rode his master's prized horse, and all went well until, on the way home, he stopped for the night at a country inn.

When Sin rose from his bed on the inn floor the next morning, his master's horse was gone. In its place there was only a poor sorry nag, as old as the Old Men of the Mountains, lame in one leg and blind in one eye. Sin was startled, unwilling to go back to his master with such a broken-down horse as that.

"I can't understand how this happened," Sin said to the innkeeper. "While on my journey, I hung a strand of hair from my horse's tail and bits of red cloth from his bridle from the spirit trees. I threw pebbles on the piles of stones that honor the spirits along the way, and I bowed to the road gods. But no doubt it was an unlucky time for me to travel. Only last night I saw a shooting star sail across the sky. That should have warned me!"

At the innkeeper's suggestion Sin set out a bowl of rice for the Spirit of the Stable where his horse had been sheltered. Bowing low over it, he cried, "Spirit of the Stable, here is my offering. Take it and eat it! And be kind enough to show me how to find my lost horse!"

But no light came to poor Sin. He next sought out a *mudang*. The sorceress cast spells. She danced and she sang in the courtyard of the inn. She beat on her drum, the waist of which was almost as thin as that of an ant. But no fine horse came galloping back into the court.

"I must seek a *pansu*!" Sin said to the innkeeper. "Only one such, who can look into both past and future, can help me in this trouble." And he sought out a blind fortuneteller and begged him to tell him where to find his lost horse.

Like all fortunetellers, this *pansu* had several ways of discovering secrets. First, he shook his little tortoise box with its eight bamboo sticks inside it. And he called to the spirits that lived in these sticks, "Good people," he cried, "be kind enough to shed your light on our darkness. Help this young man find his horse!"

When the little sticks were thrown out on the table, the *pansu* felt them all over with his clever with his fingers to discover how they'd landed. It was the same with the three coins he shook out of his little box that was shaped like a frog. Then the *pansu* said to the wide-eyed stableboy Sin, "Go! Buy a big bag of salt! Set it down before the sad animal that thief left in place of your master's fine horse. Let the horse eat all the salt it wants, but don't give it any water to drink. When the sun rises, set the sad nag free and it'll lead you to your master's horse."

Sin obeyed the wise words of the blind *pansu*. Horses love salt, so the old animal ate almost all of the pile Sin poured out before it. The sun was just giving the sky its morning brightness when Sin mounted the sorry nag and let it lead the way. Trotting along the highway to Seoul and through the crowds on the streets, it galloped straight as an arrow. Sin had to hold fast to the saddle to keep his seat on its back.

The horse finally took Sin to a village on the other side of the city. There at a certain house the animal stopped. It pushed the gate open with its impatient nose. Making straight for the water trough, the horse began drinking with great noisy gulps. Sin's eyes, however, were not fixed on that thirsty nag, but instead on his master's fine horse which stood tied in one corner of the courtyard.

"This is *my* horse," cried Sin the stableboy to the master of the house. "Give him back to me or I'll go and see the judge."

Not wanting to be punished or publicly shamed, the man returned the horse to Sin, who rode it home.

When the stableboy told his tale in his own Outer Court, all the men nodded their heads in admiration of the wisdom of the *pansu*. All of them, that is, except the old gatekeeper. "You should have thought of that scheme yourself, Sin. Every stableboy should know that people never water their horses except in their own courts. By giving salt to that nag, you made him very thirsty. Where should he have gone but back to his own drinking place? And where should you have found your master's lost horse but in the stable from which that sorry nag came?"

The Sparrows and the Flies

THE sparrows and the flies didn't like each other. They fought every day. So Hananim called them before him. "Why do you quarrel? You're a nuisance to the humans," he scolded.

"The sparrows steal rice," the flies said to Hananim. "They go into the rice fields. They eat up the grain before the harvesters can gather it. They steal straw from the roofs of houses to build their nests. And they make such a noise the people can't sleep. They're the ones who are such a nuisance!"

"That's not good. I'm sorry to hear that," Hananim replied. "The sparrows need to be punished." And without giving the birds a chance to defend themselves, he had them paddled on their poor little legs.

"*Ai-go! Ai-go!*" the sparrows cried, hopping up and down on their painful, swollen legs.

"Now let us make our case," the injured birds cried. "The flies are far worse than we are. They lay their eggs in the young rice. They spoil the good grain. They buzz in everyone's ears. They crawl on people's food. Who welcomes a fly in the early dawn when he wishes to sleep? *Ai*, the flies are even more of a nuisance to people than we are."

So Hananim ordered ordered the flies also to have a good paddling. They stood before him rubbing their forefeet together, begging that the punishments stop.

"I'll pardon you both, if it brings an end to this warfare," he said at last to the quarrelsome sparrows and flies. "Just don't forget and start fighting again. Let the sparrows always hop instead of walking like other birds! Then they'll remember the paddling they've received. Let the flies always rub their forefeet together whenever they come to rest. Thus they asked that I pardon their misdeeds."

In the end, that punishment hasn't done very much good. Sparrows and filies are still nuisances. Sparrows still steal the crops at harvest time and the flies still buzz in people's ears and still walk across their food.

The Priest and the Pigeon

A FLOCK of pigeons once made their nests beneath the eaves of a Buddhist priest's temple. The kind man fed the birds and set out water for them.

When Spring came, there were eggs in the pigeons' nests under the temple eaves. And when the eggs hatched, there were baby birds. One day a long, slinky snake crawled out from under the tiles and crawled towards the nest. Quickly before their enemy could reach the young birds, the priest struck the snake down, killing it with his walking stick.

The next afternoon, the priest set out on a journey. With his wooden begging bowl in one hand and with a sturdy staff in the other, he asked for money and food from the goodhearted people he met. When night came, he was quite a distance from the temple, so a local farmer offered him shelter in his hut, and he went into his hut. The tired priest sat down in comfort on the warm floor of the farmer's house, and he quickly drifted off to sleep.

Now one of the thankful doves from his own temple had followed the holy traveler to watch over him. While the man slept, the pigeon sat on a tree just outside the door. So it saw the snake that was silently slithering toward the farmer's house.

Somehow it knew that this was the spirit of the snake the priest had killed. It had come to get even.

"How can I warn the priest before the snake reaches him and kills him?" the pigeon thought. "My voice is too faint. I must somehow sound the temple bell. That surely will waken him."

With flapping wings, that pigeon flew back to the temple. With the help of the rest of the flock, it tugged at the immense beam used to ring the bell. But their beaks weren't strong enough. Then one of the pigeons flew with full force against the side of the bell. Boom! The sound of the metal, struck by the blow of the bird's dive, rang over the countryside. But the poor pigeon fell wounded onto the ground.

Boom went the bell again, as a second pigeon sacrificed itself for its good friend, the priest. One after the other, the birds flew against the temple bell. The priest came running up the path to find out what the matter could be, waking up just in time to escape the approaching snake bent on revenge. When he saw the poor birds lying wounded on the ground, he knew they had rung the bell and saved his life.

Clever Sim Who Would "Squeeze"

THERE once was a wise king who ruled with the help of his kindhearted minister. The minister, who unforunately wasn't exceptionally bright, appointed his cousin Sim to be governor of that province. Unlike his relative, Sim was a clever man, perhaps far too clever for his own good.

The Minister had a white horse without a dark hair on its hide. But he wasn't satisfied. He wanted a black horse, so Sim plotted to get him one. Finding a gray horse, he painted it black all over. He brushed every hair with shining black varnish, so that the horse's coat shone like the sides of a black lacquer box. It was to reward Sim for the gift of this shining black horse that the Minister gave him a province to rule over.

"I'll create a series of new taxes," Sim told himself. "I'll skim off the top and take my cut. I'll 'squeeze' wherever I can and before you know it, I'm be incredibly rich!" So squeeze he did until he indeed became wealthy. He had a huge mansion and a golden sedan chair, which eight men carried for him. He liked to ride also in his handsome single-wheeled chair, which four men guided as it rolled along over the city streets. It was quite a sight to see Sim come riding along in this one-wheeled chair. Perched high on the seat, atop the little wheeled pedestal, he looked very proud. The townspeople scurried to get out of his way. Travelers on horseback dismounted to bow as he passed. They knew he must be a very important official indeed to ride on a monocycle.

Sim squeezed out so much profit and became so rich that news of his rising fortunes made it to the King. "We need to investigate this Governor Sim," the King said to his ministers. "Send Yun to that province to bring back the truth about the squeeze he's skimming from the people."

Now Sim had a friend in the King's court, who warned him that Yun was coming, the first spy the King had sent. "This Yun is an honest man," said Sim's informer. "You can't bribe him by offering him his cut of the squeeze. But he's a timid man. He'll arrive on a sluggish mare with a suckling colt by her side."

Clever Sim easily thought of a way to make the King think that his spy, Yun, was mentally unstable. Sim's men stole the mare's colt, and they fastened a tiger's skin on its back. Then they hid it along the roadway which Yun, the spy, had to travel. When the mare came along with Yun sitting lazily upon her back, Sim's men loosed the colt in the tiger's skin. The tiger's head covered the colt's face, and the tiger's tail, stiffened with a piece of bamboo, curved over its back.

When the mare saw the colt coming towards her, she smelled only the tiger's skin. Turning tail, she immediately galloped back to the capital, fleeing along the road, through the streets and into the palace court. Yun tried his best to keep his seat on the frightened mare, and the colt, looking for all the world like a tiger, bounded behind.

Everyone fled in panic from this curious beast, until the colt began to drink its mother's milk. The courtiers burst into loud laughter at the sight of a mare suckling a tiger. The King, think-

ing Yun had played this trick himself, exiled him to the lonely island called Quelpart.

"Send Sun this time. He's not as foolish as Yun," the King next commanded. And soon Sim received warning of the coming of this second spy, who would report to the King about Sim's squeezing habit. "This spy, Sun, isn't timid. He rides a white mule, and there's no colt. But he dearly loves drinking wine and listening to women sing."

So at every inn Sim stationed *gesangs*, the very best singers he could find in his province. They filled the spy's wine bowls again and again. They delayed him as long as they could with their beautiful songs and their graceful dances. It was when the spy was in the finest of all these inns that Sim played the best of his tricks on Sun.

A feast had been laid out for the spy, while the innkeeper's wife gave him gave him wine and entertained him. "The only danger to you, Honorable Guest," the young woman warned Sun, "is my husband's homecoming. The master of this inn is a jealous man. When he comes and finds you still here with me, you will do well to hide."

So when the innkeeper returned, the spy gladly crawled into a great cash box. The woman snapped the huge brass lock shut, pushing its great prongs firmly into their socket. The innkeeper also played his part well. He pretended to be angry, and the spy inside the box trembled when he heard his tirade. "Where is that traveler?" the man scolded his wife. "His white mule is outside. I know you've hidden him. If you have, I'll turn you out of this house right now!"

"But how shall we divide all the things we own together," the woman said, also pretending to be angry. They quarreled and quarreled, but they succeeded in dividing up everything, except the cash box, which they both claimed. At last, much to his horror, the prisoner inside heard the man say, "We'll just have to saw the cash box in two."

"It's far too fine a chest for that," the wife objected. "We'll take it to the judge." The spy was relieved to have escaped death from a saw, but he was sure he would be paddled if the chest were opened up before the judge.

"I cannot decide this question with fairness," said Governor Sim, who played the part of the judge. "But I'll give you two hundred coins for it, and I'll keep it myself." So the innkeeper and his wife went back home, well rewarded for their bit of playacting.

Sim loaded the cash box between carrying poles and sent it to the King. Speaking loudly so that the spy, Sun, would be able to hear him, he said to the porters, "Drop this chest in the river if you hear any noises that sound as though there are spirits inside." The terrified spy didn't make a peep until the chest was at last set down before the King and his ministers.

The ministers roared with laughter when the box was unlocked and poor Sun was dumped out! His legs were so cramped from the long ride that he could only crawl about on all fours like a turtle.

"Surely this is another trick," the King concluded and sent Sun to Quelpart too.

But Sim wasn't in the clear. "Kun, a third spy, is about to arrive," his friend wrote to him. "He never drinks wine, and he prefers temple bells to *gesangs'* singing. And he isn't timid at all. He stands in awe only of the shaven-headed priests of the temple."

Clever Sim was not long in planning a way to trick this man, too. When Kun arrived at the halfway inn, he heard the sounds of strange temple music from up on the hillside. "It's the gods assembling on their sacred mountain," the innkeeper told him, following Governor Sim's orders. "They come here only once in a thousand years. Only very good people are allowed to visit them there."

The pious messenger, Kun, trembled with excitement. "I'll go to the temple and worship the Great Buddha. Perhaps then the gods will receive me."

So Kun climbed the mountain, just as Sim had intended him to do. There in a dell he found four old men dressed in long flowing robes, and there were four young boys, also in curious clothing, waiting on the old men and handing round wine. Urged by the mountain gods, Kun drank from each bowl. The wine was strong, and he soon fell into a sound sleep.

Before he awoke, Sim's men dressed him in tattered clothing. They put a rotting stick in the place of his staff, and they carried him off far into the high mountains.

Next morning when Kun again came to his senses, he thought at first he'd been taken by the gods to Heaven itself. But quickly seeing this wasn't the case, he started down the mountain again. As if by accident, a man gathering brushwood came up the path. "Tell me, good sir," poor Kun inquired of him. "Have you heard what became of the King's messenger, Kun, who was yesterday at the inn?"

"There was such a one, I have been told," the woodcutter replied. "But they say he was carried off by the gods two hundred years ago."

"That heavenly wine must have put me to sleep," the befuddled Kun said to himself, "I've slept for two hundred years.

That's why my clothes are so tattered, why my staff has rotted away, why the King's seal is so rusted."

Shaking his head in dismay, he went back to the inn where he heard the same story. The innkeeper brought him fresh clothing without any holes. He found him a chair and some bearers to carry him home. To Kun's surprise, his own family looked just as they had when he had started out on his journey. So did the King and the King's minister.

"You haven't changed a bit in two hundred years," Kun exclaimed to the King. And when he insisted he had drunk with the gods, they declared he was crazy. Kun, too, was sent to join the other two spies on the faraway island of Quelpart in the south.

As for Sim, the King never gave up trying to stop him from squeezing. "He is far too clever to be caught," he said to the Minister. "We'd best bring him back here to the court. We can set him the task of calming those people who clamor for favors at our palace gate."

So Sim used his clever tricks to turn these pests against one another. They fought so much that they forgot to pester the King with their complaints. In the end, Sim was made the King's treasurer, so he could keep squeezing as much as he liked without stealing from the poor.

The Tiger Hunter
and the Mirror

PIL the tiger hunter had killed a ferocious beast that had been terrorizing the countryside for ages. This was no ordinary tiger but had white whiskers as long as a human hand and fur as soft and thick as the finest silk. Its teeth were as sharp as needles and its jaws wide enough to carry off a grown man.

There was great fanfare in Pil's court when the King's messengers came. Nothing so splendid as their fine feathered hats and their bright red-and-green robes had ever been seen there. In the great chest they carried were rich gifts to reward the hunter who had freed the people from this vicious scourge. There were silks of many colors, green as the young rice plants, red as the red peppers, and blue as the sky. There were fans and a long pipe with a carved silver bowl. But, strangest of all, was a silver mirror.

Although Pil was an accomplished hunter, he was a simple man, and his family, like him, were all countryfolk. They knew almost nothing about city ways. They'd never seen a shining silver disk like the one Pil lifted out of the King's treasure chest.

Pil's wife was the first to look closely at the clear surface of the silver mirror, and she gave a loud cry. "*Ai-go! Ai-go!*" she wailed when she saw a woman's face, her own, staring back at her. "Here my husband has brought home a second wife to take my place. Or perhaps she's a singing girl. That is much worse. Whoever she is, I'll not have her in my house." Of course never having owned a mirror before, this woman had never really seen her own face, except in the dull waters of the stream where she washed the family clothes.

Pil came running to find out what was the matter. He, too, peered intently into the mirror. Naturally, the face he saw there was that of a man, and he, too, flew into a rage, screaming "Who is that man? My wife has hidden a stranger in our Inner Court."

The hubbub brought the tiger hunter's old mother hurrying to see what was the matter. When she looked into the magic silver disk, she saw, of course, a face covered with wrinkles and topped with gray hair. It was for all the world like that of her troublesome neighbor who was always borrowing food. "*Ai*, here is that beggar from down the road," she said under her breath. She couldn't understand why, when she turned around, she found nobody there.

The grandfather, in his turn, thought the face he saw in the mirror was that of the old *pansu* who had come to demand payment for choosing a grave site. "How did that *pansu* make his way into our house without somebody seeing him?" and "Where has he gone now?" he cried, looking for the intruder both inside the house and in the courtyard.

The story of the strange object in Pil's house spread throughout the village. The neighbors gathered, and all tried to solve the problem in vain. There were many loud arguments as each one saw his own unfamiliar face in the mirror.

Even the village judge couldn't understand the round silver disk. When he saw the head of a man, capped with his own judge's hat, staring out at him, he began to complain. "Why is there another judge sent here from the Capital?" he scolded. "Haven't I done an excellent job? Call out the tiger hunters! Let them drive this strange judge away from our peaceful village!"

Happily, the messengers had not yet ridden back to the King's court. They roared with laughter when they learned of the commotion this royal gift of a mirror had caused!

"Ho! Ho! Ho!" they laughed. "Ha! Ha! Ha! Ho! Ho! Ho!" "Honorable Judge," they said to the village elder, "it's you yourself reflected in that mirror." They explained how the shining metal gave back the face of him who looked into it.

"Ho! Ho! Ho!" Pil laughed louder than anyone else at the joke at his expense. His wife joined in, happy she had no cause to be jealous of a second woman under her roof. "Ho! Ho! Ho!" Similarly the villagers burst into laughter whenever they looked into their own mirrors—for, of course, each household now had to have at least one of these amazing "looking glasses." And the tiger hunter Pil was the man they chose to ride on a fine horse to the King's city to buy them.

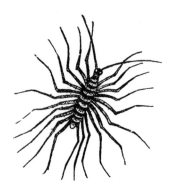

The Rooster and
the Centipede

THERE once was a young and courteous man who earned his rice by finding customers for an important silk merchant. He was so polite and convincing that when he stood on the street hawking the merchant's wares, curious customers flocked to the silk shop.

"Buy silk! Fine silk! No better silk in all the land!" Chu was crying this one day when the maidservant of a rich widow walked by. Under his influence, she bought the best silk the shop offered, and she paid for her purchase with shining gold coins out of her embroidered belt pocket.

Not many days later, the maidservant came to the Street of Silk Merchants again. Though young men from other silk shops begged her to enter, she waited for Chu. And again she bought yards and yards of silk. A third time then a fourth time she came to the shop. The merchant was pleased, and it meant good earnings for Chu too.

One afternoon the widow's maidservant politely requested Chu to accompany her home. Her mistress wished to talk with him about some special silk she wished to buy for a screen. Now this lady was a widow, and Chu himself was a widower, his young wife having died when the Spirit of Smallpox entered his courts. Both were young. Both were attractive. Before long, the two were married, and the young man went to live with her in her lavish home.

All went well. Chu was happy. Never had he known so kind and so pleasant a woman as his new wife. He had fine coats of silk, and each meal was as bountiful as an Ancestors' Feast.

While out on his walks, Chu usually crossed the Chicken Bridge near his home. One evening, while crossing the bridge, he heard a voice calling his name. "Chu, Chu, my son!" the voice said. "This is your father warning you of danger. That person in your house, that woman, brings you bad luck. You must put her to death. Crush her as you would a centipede that crawls near your foot."

"How should I kill my beautiful wife?" Chu replied to the voice that came from under the bridge. "She is good. She is kind. She has brought me only good luck. I could never do her harm." And he went on his way.

The next time the young man crossed over the Chicken Bridge, the voice of his dead father came to him again. "Kill that person in your house, my son. Your father's spirit commands you. She is a demon in woman's form. If she doesn't die before the fifteenth of this month, then your own spirit will ride the winds to join me here on the Distant Shore."

Now the young man was troubled. The voice that gave him this dire command sounded just like that of his own father. He was a good son who always had obeyed the words of his parents. But when he thought of the comfort and kindness which he received from his wife, he knew he could never harm her.

With a heavy heart, on the fifteenth of the month, the hours dragged by. That evening, he entered the inner court where his wife didn't move towards him as usual. She only sat on the soft white mat on the floor, as if lost in a dream.

As Chu watched in silence, her face turned first to dead white, then to pale green. The woman began to groan and to shiver. Chu was spellbound. He didn't dare touch her or call out her name, for he could see she was bewitched. At last, his wife emerged from her disturbing trance. Chu was overjoyed to see her skin clear. She opened her eyes and began to speak to him.

"Why didn't you kill me, as the voice under the bridge commanded you, Master of my House?"

"What are you saying? Why would you ask me that?" Chu replied. "How did you know about the voice under the bridge?"

"I will tear the paper out of the windowpane of your understanding so that you may see clearly into the heart of that curious happening under the bridge," Chu's wife said to him. "It is a strange story, but it has a golden ending. By your kindness and your faithfulness you have released me from a terrible prison.

"You must know that, in an earlier life, the Jade Emperor of Heaven decided to punish me for some misdoing. He changed me from a woman into a centipede, then he sent a rooster to torment me. Through one life after another, that rooster has pursued me. Only after a thousand years was I permitted to take on my former shape and become a woman again. But still my enemy followed me.

"Once I'd returned to a woman's form, I was too large and strong for the rooster to kill all by himself. So the only hope was to persuade some man to perform the dreadful deed for him. It was the rooster's voice you heard, my husband, imitating your dead father. And it was your good heart that kept you from obeying that false command.

"Today marks the last day of the amount of time given to the rooster to kill me. My spirit was fighting with his spirit when you came into the Inner Court this afternoon. As you see, I won the battle. Now I'm free of him forever. Now I can remain a woman and your wife. Peace lies before us."

The next morning, when Chu came to the Chicken Bridge, he climbed down to the spot the strange voice had emantated from. There on the ground he found an enormous old white rooster as tall as Yong Tu. But the rooster was dead, and never again did Chu's wife have to live in fear. Still, to this day, a rooster will pounce on a centipede whenever it sees one.

The Story Bag

THERE once lived a very rich family. They had only one child, a boy, who loved to have stories told to him. Whenever he met a new person, he'd say, "Tell me a story!"

Whenever he was told a new tale, he'd store it in a small bag he carried at his belt. Eventually he'd heard so many stories that the bag was packed tight and he had to push hard to get each new story in. To make sure that none of the stories escaped, he kept the bag tied tightly at the top.

The boy eventually grew into a handsome young man. The time came for him to take a wife. A bride was chosen for him, and the whole house was preparing to greet the young master's new wife. Everything was in an uproar.

There happened to be in this rich home a faithful old servant who'd been with the family ever since the story-loving boy was still very young. As the household made ready for the young master's wedding, this servant was tending a fire on the kitchen hearth. Suddenly his ears caught faint whispering sounds coming from somewhere. He listened carefully and soon discovered that the voices were coming from a bag hanging on the wall. It was the bag of stories which the young master had kept in his childhood. Now it hung forgotten on an old nail on the kitchen wall. The old servant listened carefully.

"Listen, everyone," said a voice, "the wedding is to take place tomorrow. He's kept us stuffed in this bag all this time, packed together with no room. We've suffered long enough! It's time to make him pay one way or another!"

"Yes," said another voice, "I've been thinking the same thing. Tomorrow the young man will leave by horse to bring home his bride. I'll change into bright red berries, ripening by the roadside. There I'll wait for him. I'll be poisonous but will also look so beautiful that he'll want to eat me. If he does, I'll claim his life."

"If he doesn't die after eating the berries," piped up a third voice, "I'll become a clear, bubbling spring by the roadside. I'll have a beautiful gourd dipper floating in me. When he sees me he'll be thirsty and will drink me. Once he's swallowed me, I'll make him suffer terribly."

A fourth voice then broke in: "If you fail, then I'll become an iron skewer, heated red-hot, and I'll hide in the bag of chaff that will be placed by his horse for him to dismount when he reaches

his bride's home. And when he steps on me, I'll burn his feet badly." Because, you see, according to the custom of the land in those days, a bag of chaff was always placed by the bridegroom's horse so that he wouldn't have to step directly on the ground.

Then a fifth voice whispered: "If that fails too, I'll become those poisonous string-snakes, thin as threads. Then I'll hide in the bridal chamber. When the bride and the bridegroom have gone to sleep, I'll come out and bite them."

The servant was alarmed to hear these threats. "This is terrible," he told himself. "I mustn't let any harm come to the young master. When he leaves the house tomorrow, I must take the bridle and lead the horse myself."

Early next morning, the final preparations were completed, and the wedding procession was ready to set forth. The groom, dressed in his best, came out of the house and mounted his horse. Suddenly the faithful servant came running out and grabbed the horse's bridle. He then asked to be allowed to lead the horse.

The old master of the house said: "You have other work to do. You had better stay behind."

"But I *must* lead the horse today," the servant said. "I don't care what happens, but I insist that I take the bridle."

He refused to listen to anyone and, finally, the master, surprised at the old man's obstinacy, allowed him to lead the horse to the bride's home.

As the procession wound along its way, the bridegroom came to an open field. Bright berries were growing along the road. They looked temptingly delicious.

"Wait!" the bridegroom called out. "Stop the horse and pick me some of those berries."

But the servant wouldn't stop, instead purposely making the horse pick up speed. "Those berries," he said, "can be found anywhere. Just be patient. I'll pick some for you later." And he gave the horse a good crack of the whip.

After a while, they came to a bubbling spring. Its clear waters were cool and tempting. There was even a small gourd dipper

floating on the water, as if to invite the passerby to have a drink.

"Bring me some of that water," the bridegroom said to the servant. "I'm really thirsty!"

But, again, the servant prodded the horse and hurried by. "Once we get into the shade of those trees, your thirst will soon disappear," he said, and he gave the horse another crack of the whip, a blow much harder than the first.

The bridegroom grumbled and mumbled from atop his horse. He was in a bad mood, but the servant took no notice. He only made the horse hurry the faster.

Soon they reached the bride's home. There, already gathered in the yard, was a large crowd of people. The servant led the horse into the compound and stopped it beside the waiting bag of chaff. As the bridegroom put down his foot to dismount, the servant pretended to stumble and shoved the bridegroom to keep him from stepping on the bag.

The bridegroom fell but couldn't scold the servant in front of the guests. So he held his tongue and entered the bride's home.

There, the wedding ceremony was held without untoward incident, and the newly-married couple returned to the groom's home.

Soon night fell, and the bride and bridegroom retired to their room. The faithful servant armed himself with a sword and hid himself under the veranda outside the bridal chamber.

As soon as the bride and bridegroom turned out the lights and went to bed, the servant opened the door of the room and leapt inside.

The newly-wed couple were startled beyond description. "Who's there?" they both shouted, jumping out of bed.

"Young master," the servant said, "I shall explain later. Right now, just hurry and get out of the way."

The servant kicked the bedding aside and lifted the mattress. A terrible sight greeted their eyes. There hundreds of string-snakes coiled and writhed in a single ball. The servant slashed at the snakes with the sword in his hand. As he cut some into pieces, they opened their red mouths and darted their black forked tongues at him. Other snakes slithered here and there, trying to escape the servant's flashing sword. The servant whirled here and there like a madman and finally killed every one of the snakes in the room.

He let out a sign of relief and began: "Young master, this is the story…" And the old servant recounted the whispers he'd heard coming from the old bag on the kitchen wall.

That is why when stories are heard they must never be stored away to become mean and spiteful. Instead, they should always be shared with other people. In this way, they are passed from one person to another so that as many people can enjoy them!

The Pheasant, the Dove,
and the Magpie

A pheasant, a dove and a magpie all lived in the same forest. One year the crops failed, and there was nothing for the three of them to eat.

"What shall we do? How can we live through this cold winter?" The three talked over their problems and finally decided to call on a mouse who also lived in the same forest. "Surely," they said, "the mouse will have some rice and will share it with us." They decided that the pheasant would go first to see the mouse.

The pheasant was always a proud bird and until then had looked down on the lowly mouse. So when he came to the home of the mouse, he spoke rudely out of habit.

"Hey there!" the pheasant said haughtily, "where are you? It's me, the one and only! Bring me some food!"

Mrs. Mouse was in the kitchen at the back of the house, feeding fuel into her kitchen stove. When she heard the disdainful words of the pheasant, she became very angry. She flew out of the kitchen, a red-hot poker in her hand, and began hitting the pheasant on both his cheeks.

"How dare you speak to us like that when you've come begging for food. Even if we had rice to throw away, we wouldn't give you any."

Rubbing his red and swollen cheeks, the pheasant ran home in shame. That's why, to this day, the pheasant's cheeks are red.

Next the dove went to the mouse's home. He, too, was a very proud bird and looked down on the mouse.

"Say, you rice thief! I've come for a bit of food," he said in a rude and haughty manner.

Mrs. Mouse became angry again when she heard the dove speak so rudely. She ran out of her kitchen with a poker in her hand and konked the dove on top of his head.

Ever since then, the top of a dove's head has always been blue. It is the bruise that was caused by Mrs. Mouse and her poker.

Lastly, the magpie went to get some food. The magpie knew too well what had happened to his two friends, the pheasant and the dove. He didn't want to make the same mistake, so he decided to be very, very careful how he spoke.

As soon as he reached the front door of Mr. Mouse's home, he bowed humbly and spoke as politely as possible. "My dear Mr. Mouse," he said, "we have had a very poor harvest and I am in want. Can you not spare me a little food?"

Mr. Mouse came to the front door. "Well, Mr. Magpie, I won't say that I wouldn't give you anything. But aren't you a crony of the pheasant and the dove? If you are, then I'll certainly have nothing to do with you."

"Oh no, Mr. Mouse," said the magpie, "absolutely not. I've never even heard of them."

"In that case, come in," the mouse said, believing what the magpie told him. The mouse then gave the magpie some rice to take home.

On top of all this, Mrs. Mouse, her good mood restored, said: "Mr. Magpie, you certainly are a refined gentleman with a gift for gab. You must've had a very good upbringing."

And so, to this day, the magpie is known for his cunning and slyness.

The Bad Tiger

IN a great forest there once lived a very bad tiger. Every night he would come out of his lair and steal into a radish patch kept by a poor old woman. There the bad tiger would trample all over the garden, eating the choicest and fattest radishes.

The poor woman came every morning to her radish patch and cried at the damage the tiger had caused. She didn't know what to do, for the tiger was as strong as he was bad. She wondered and wondered how she could stop the tiger from eating her radishes every night. Finally, she hit on a plan.

One day, she met the tiger and said: "Mr. Tiger, why do you have to eat radishes all the time? Please come to my house, and I shall make some delicious, nourishing red-bean gruel for you to eat."

The tiger was overjoyed at the prospect of a red-bean gruel, for it was his favorite dish. "Thank you. I'll be over tonight," he said, licking his chops at the thought of the feast.

The old woman hurried home to prepare for the tiger's arrival. First she lit a fire and heated up a large mass of charcoal. She put the glowing coals in a brazier and took the brazier outside to the back of her home.

Then, she floated some red-hot cayenne pepper on the water in her kitchen jug.

Next, she stuck a large number of needles into the kitchen towel.

She then scattered cow dung all around the kitchen door, and spread a large straw mat, used in drying unhulled rice, out in the yard.

Finally, she brought out an A-frame, used on the back when carrying heavy loads and shaped like the letter "A" turned upside down. She propped the A-frame up against the back fence.

Now everything was ready. The old woman went back to her kitchen and, as though nothing was out of the ordinary, pretended she was preparing the evening dinner.

Soon it was dark, and the bad tiger came sneaking to her house. The old woman heard the tiger outside and said: "Oh, it's you, Mr. Tiger. Please do come in." And she opened the front door, smiling to welcome her guest.

"My, it's cold tonight, isn't it, Mr. Tiger?" she said. "You won't mind, will you, bringing the charcoal brazier into the house from the back for me?"

"Of course," the bad tiger said, for he was in a good mood thinking of the feast he was about to have.

He went out back and was about to lift the brazier up when he noticed that the charcoal was almost out. "Say, old woman. The charcoal is almost out. There are hardly any red embers left."

The old woman answered from inside the house: "Is that so? Will you blow on the embers for me and heat up the coals again?"

The bad tiger put his nose to the brazier and puffed and puffed. He blew so hard that some ashes whirled up and dropped into his eyes. He rubbed and rubbed them, but the more he did,

the more they hurt. In intense pain, the tiger cried: "Old woman, old woman! I've got some ashes in my eyes. Help me!"

"My, I'm sorry," she said. "Try washing your eyes with water. You'll find some in the kitchen jug there."

So the tiger did as he was told, and started gulping the water with the cayenne pepper floating on top. It got in both his eyes, so he was in even greater pain than before. He thought he'd surely go blind.

"Old woman, old woman!" he called, "my eyes are worse than before. What can I do?" the tiger moaned, pressing his eyes with his front paws and stamping his feet in pain.

"Is it that painful? Try wiping them with this kitchen towel."

The bad tiger was in great pain. So the tiger grabbed the towel she handed him and began rubbing his eyes frantically. But the needles pricked his eyes. The tiger was now in so much pain, he couldn't stand it.

Suddenly the tiger realized how he'd been tricked by the old woman. Blindly he tried to run away. But as soon as he stepped out the kitchen door, he slipped on the cow dung and fell head over heels on the ground.

The straw mat, which the old woman had laid out in the back yard, came flying through the air. It quickly wrapped the bad tiger in a tight roll.

Next, the A-frame emerged from the back fence and threw the tightly wrapped tiger on its back. Then, without a word, it ran right down to the sea and threw the bad tiger headlong into the waves.

That was the end of the bad tiger. Thereafter the old woman was able to raise her radishes in peace. There was no longer a bad tiger to come and dig up her radish patch.

The Three Little Girls

DEEP in the mountains was a lonely hut where a mother and her three small daughters lived. The eldest girl was named Haisuni, the second Talsuni, and the youngest Peolsuni.

One day the mother had to leave home to take some firewood to a distant market to sell. Before she left she called her three daughters and said: "Listen, Haisuni, Talsuni, and Peolsuni. Do be careful while I'm gone as there's a ferocious tiger roaming the woods nearby. Don't open the door to anybody until I get back. Otherwise you might be eaten by the savage beast."

Giving her warning, the mother stepped out the door and went on her way.

Just as she was leaving, the bad tiger happened to pass the house. He was very hungry and was in search of food. He saw the mother leave the house and thought: "Ho ho! Now's my chance! Now that the mother's gone, I'll be able to eat those three young girls of hers. They should make a tasty dinner for me. How nice that would be!"

The tiger waited a while to make sure that the mother didn't return. Then, when he thought the time was ripe, he crept up to the house and called out in his sweetest voice: "Haisuni, Talsuni, Peolsuni—Mother has just come back. Please open the door."

Of course, no matter how sweetly the tiger spoke, his voice was not the voice of their mother. So the eldest girl, Haisuni, asked: "Is that really you, Mother? It doesn't sound a bit like you."

"Why, of course I'm your mother," the tiger answered. "I was invited to a feast and there I sang so many songs that my voice has become hoarse."

The second daughter, Talsuni, then asked: "If you are really our mother, then show us your eyes. We would be able to tell for sure."

Hearing this, the tiger put his blood-shot eyes to a knothole in the front door and peered into the house.

Talsuni saw the red eyes and drew back in surprise. "Oh my! Why are your eyes so red?"

The tiger, a bit confused, hurriedly explained: "I dropped in at Grandfather's house and helped grind some red pepper pods. Some of the pepper got into my eyes, and that's why they are so red."

The third daughter, Peolsuni, next asked: "If that's true, then let us see your hands. We could really tell then whether you are our mother or not."

The tiger put his hairy, yellow paws to a chink in the door.

Peolsuni peeked through the crack and cried: "Why! Your hands are all yellow!"

"Yes, my child," the tiger said, "I was helping our relatives in the next village plaster their house with yellow mud. That's why my hands are so yellow."

In this way the clever tiger fooled all the girls completely. The three sisters, sure that it was their mother, unlocked the front door. And who should come in but a huge, yellow tiger!

"My, you children looked after the house well, didn't you?" the tiger said. "As a reward, Mother will cook a nice dinner for you." The tiger went into the kitchen, his eyes shining with greed.

The three girls stood huddled in a corner, quivering with fear. "What should we do? The tiger has tricked us and now he'll eat us all!"

The three girls quickly ran out of the house. Then tiptoeing softly away, they quickly climbed up a pine tree growing near the well. There they hid quietly in the branches.

The tiger soon noticed that the girls were no longer in the house. "Haisuni, Talsuni, Peolsuni," he called, "where are you?"

The tiger looked everywhere, inside and outside the house, but he still couldn't find the girls. Then he passed the well and happened to glance in. There he saw in the water the reflection of the three girls hiding in the branches of the pine tree.

"Children, children," he purred. "What are you doing up there? I want to come up too, but it looks difficult. Tell Mother how to climb the tree."

At this, Haisuni called down: "There's some sesame oil in the kitchen cupboard. Rub some of the oil on the trunk of the tree. Then you can easily climb up."

Quickly, the tiger went into the house, got the oil, and rubbed it on the trunk of the tree. Then he tried to climb, but the oil made him slip all the more, and try as he might, he could not reach the girls.

Once again, the tiger looked up into the tree and said: "Be good children, dears, and tell me truly how to climb the tree."

Talsuni, the second daughter, unthinkingly let her tongue slip and said: "There's an ax in the shed. If you cut some notches in the tree trunk, then you can climb up."

Quickly, the tiger went for the ax and began cutting footholds with it. One step at a time, he climbed up and up toward the girls.

The three sisters were desperate. They were sure they'd be eaten up. They raised their eyes toward the sky and prayed to the God of Heaven. "Please help us. Send down your golden bucket," they prayed.

Their prayers were answered, and from the top of a cloud down came a golden bucket. The three sisters climbed into the bucket and were lifted up, out of the teeth of danger, into the clouds.

When the tiger saw this, he too prayed: "Please send down a bucket for me also."

Once again, a well bucket came down from the clouds. But this time, the rope of the bucket was old and rotten. The tiger, nevertheless, climbed into the bucket, and it started to rise. When he was halfway up to the cloud, the rope suddenly broke, and the tiger came crashing to earth, right in the middle of a millet field.

That's why the tops of the millet are mottled to this day. The reddish spots are from the blood of the tiger which splattered all over the millet field.

As to the three sisters who climbed to Heaven, they were each given a special task. Haisuni was made to shine in the sky during the day. Talsuni was made to shine at night. And Peolsuni was to twinkle on nights when Talsuni slept or was on her way from the sky to rest. That is why the sun is called Haisuni, the moon Talsuni, and the stars Peolsuni. To this very day, the three sisters take turns brightening the world with their light.

The Deer and the Woodcutter

LONG, long ago, a poor woodcutter lived with his mother at the foot of the Kumgang Mountains. Every day he would go into the mountains to cut wood, for that was his job.

One fine autumn day, when the red maple trees flamed everywhere, the woodcutter went as usual to chop wood in the forest. He was hard at work when a stately deer came running out of the forest. He was panting and seemed almost on the point of collapsing from exhaustion.

"Save me, please!" the deer cried, "a hunter is chasing me." And he looked back in fear, as if expecting the hunter to come out of the woods at any moment.

The woodcutter felt sorry for the deer and said: "Here, I'll help you. Quick, hide under these branches."

The woodcutter covered the deer with a small tree he'd just cut down. No sooner had he hidden the deer than a hunter appeared carrying a gun.

"Say!" the hunter said. "Didn't a deer come running this way?"

"Yes," the woodcutter answered with a straight face, "but he kept on going that way."

The hunter quickly ran in the direction the woodcutter had pointed.

After the hunter was gone, the deer emerged from its hiding spot. "I can't thank you enough," he said. "You saved my life. I'll never forget your kindness." The deer thanked the woodcutter many, many times and then disappeared into the forest.

Some days later the deer came again to where the woodcutter was working and said: "I've come today to repay you for saving my life. Don't you want to have a beautiful wife?"

The woodcutter blushed. "Of course I do. But who would marry a poor man like me?"

"Don't say that. Just listen to me. If you do as I say, you'll meet the perfect partner this very day. All you have to do is…" Then the deer put his mouth to the woodcutter's ears and began whispering: "If you cross that divide and go straight on, you will come to a large pond. Often beautiful fairies come down from Heaven to bathe in that pool. They're sure to be there today. If you start out now, you'll be able to see them. When you get there, take just one of the robes which the fairies have hung on the trees while they bathe, and hide it carefully. Remember, take only one. Their robes are made of very fine feathers, and without them the fairies can't fly back to Heaven. So one of the fairies will be left without her robe. Take that fairy home, and she'll become your bride. Do you understand? Remember, take only one robe. You'll surely succeed, *so* leave right away."

The woodcutter listened carefully, but he found the deer's story hard to believe.

"Don't worry," the deer said. "Just do exactly as I said."

At this, the woodcutter decided to give it a try. "I'll go and see," he said.

As he started out, the deer called him back and said: "Oh, there is one more thing. After the fairy has become your bride,

you must be very careful until she has given birth to four children. No matter how she may ask, you must never bring out her robe of feathers nor show it to her. If you do, there will be nothing but trouble."

The woodcutter climbed straight up the path the deer had shown him. He crossed the mountain divide and, sure enough, presently he came to a large pond. And in the pond, he saw a number of fairies bathing, looking as if they'd stepped out of a painting. Hanging on the trees were many, many shining robes of feathers, as light and thin as gossamer.

"So these are the robes of feathers the deer spoke about," thought the woodcutter. Quietly, he took one from a tree and folded it over and over. The robe was so thin that, when it was folded, it was no thicker than a piece of paper. The woodcutter then carefully hid the robe in his breast pocket. Then he sat down in the shade of a nearby tree and watched the fairies from a distance.

When the fairies finished bathing, they came up from the pond to put on their robes. They each had a robe, except for one fairy. Her robe was gone! She looked everywhere, but she couldn't find it. The other fairies grew worried, and they too joined in the search. They looked high and low, but the robe was nowhere.

After a long while, the sun began to set, and the fairies said: "We can't keep looking forever. If it gets too late, the gates of Heaven will be closed. We'll have to leave you here alone, but when we get back to Heaven we'll talk with the others and try to do something to help you." Then they spread out the hems of their robes and flew up into the sky, leaving the one poor fairy all by herself beside the pond.

So the fairy missing her feathered robe was taken home by the poor woodcutter and became his bride.

The two were very happy, and the woodcutter counted himself very fortunate. Once the fairy had become the woodcutter's wife, she seemed to forget all about returning to Heaven, as she settled into life in her new home. She cared faithfully for her mother-in-law and for her husband. Then one, two, three children were born to them, and she raised the children with loving care.

The woodcutter soon lost all fear that his wife might one day leave him. She never once mentioned the robe of feathers, and the woodcutter didn't breathe a word of it either. But he never forgot what the deer warned, that he mustn't show his wife the robe until four children were born.

One evening after a hard day's work, the woodcutter was seated at home, drinking the wine his wife was serving him with loving care.

"I never knew that the world of man was such a pleasant place to live in," his wife remarked casually. "I wouldn't even dream of returning to Heaven. But isn't it strange? I often wonder where my robe of feathers disappeared to. Could it be possible that you hid it?"

The woodcutter was an honest man at heart. So when his wife asked him about the robe, he couldn't bring himself to feign ignorance. Besides, his wife had given birth to their three children. How could he lie to her? The rice wine, too, had gone slightly to his head, and he was caught off guard.

"I've kept it a secret until now," he said, "but you're right. I'm the one who hid your robe."

"Oh," she answered with a smile, "so it *was* you, after all. I often thought it might be so. When I think of the past, I feel a pang of yearning for old things. I wonder how the robe looks after all these years. Please let me take a look at it for a moment."

Somehow, the woodcutter felt relieved at having told his wife the secret he had kept hidden all to himself these many years. Forgetting all about the deer's warning, he gladly brought out the robe and showed it to her.

His wife spread the beautiful robe in her hands, and, as she did so, a strange and indescribable feeling stirred in her heart. A snatch of an old song rose to her lips:

> *The multi-colored clouds now spread,*
> *Gold and silver, purple and red;*
> *And the strains of a heavenly sound*
> *In the balmy skies redound.....*

From the robe of feathers held in her hands, memories of dreamy days living in Heaven now returned with startling clarity, and she was filled with an uncontrollable homesickness.

Suddenly she placed the robe lightly on her shoulders. Then she put one child on her back and the other two under each arm.

"Farewell, my husband," she said, "I must, after all, go back to Heaven." And with these words she rose into the air.

The woodcutter was so astounded that at first he couldn't move. When he was finally able to run outside, his wife was floating high in the sky like a tiny dragonfly winging its way to Heaven.

No matter how much the woodcutter regretted his mistake, it was too late. He no longer had the will to go to work. Every day he stayed at home, staring into the sky, missing his wife and children.

One day the deer he'd saved appeared at the woodcutter's door. The deer already knew that the woodcutter's wife had returned to Heaven, taking with her the three children.

"Didn't I tell you so?" the deer said. "If there had been four children, this would never have happened. You see, a mother can't leave a child behind. If you'd had four children, she couldn't have carried the fourth and so couldn't have left you."

Hearing the deer's words, the woodcutter felt even more ashamed of himself. All he could do was hang his head and continue sighing.

"But," the deer continued, "don't be too disheartened. There is still a way you can be reunited with her. You remember that pond, don't you? Since the day the robe was lost, the fairies no longer come down to earth. Instead, they send down a bucket on a rope from Heaven and draw up water from that pond. Apparently the water of that pond is better even than the water in Heaven.

"Now, this is what you should do. Go to the pond and wait. When the bucket is lowered and filled with water, hurry and empty it out. Then climb inside the bucket yourself, and you will be drawn up into Heaven."

Again the woodcutter did as the deer told him and gained

entrance to Heaven where he was reunited with his wife and children. His wife was once again a fairy, but she was overjoyed to see her husband and greeted him with open arms.

Many, many happy days followed for them. The woodcutter's life in Heaven was like a dream. Heaven was beautiful beyond belief. Never had the woodcutter seen or even imagined such beautiful scenery. Every day was an ecstasy of delight.

Still, there was one thing that troubled him. He often thought of his mother, whom he had left behind in the village at the foot of the Kumgang Mountains. Time and time again, he asked himself: "I wonder what Mother is doing now? She surely must be lonely, living all by herself." And every time he thought of his mother, he kept saying: "If I could only see her just once, I would be very, very happy."

His wife, the fairy, said: "If you're so worried about her, why don't you go to see her? I'll bring you a heavenly horse, which will take you to Mother's place in an instant." So she brought him a heavenly horse.

As her husband was mounting the horse, the fairy said: "Listen! There is one important thing to remember. You must never get off this horse. If you so much as set a single foot on the ground, you will never be able to return to Heaven. Whatever happens, don't ever dismount. Do everything that you must do sitting on the horse." Only after the fairy had repeated this instruction over and over again did she finally allow her husband to set out on his journey.

As soon as the woodcutter was firmly mounted, the heavenly horse whinnied once and was off like a bolt of lightning. In no time at all they reached the village at the foot of the Kumgang Mountains.

The woodcutter's mother had been living a lonely life all alone. When she saw her son atop a horse at her door, she wept with joy.

But her son wouldn't get off his horse. "Mother," he said, "I'm so glad to see you well. Please take good care of yourself and stay strong and well forever. If I get off this horse, I cannot go back to Heaven, and so I must say farewell from here." The woodcutter then pulled on the reins and was about to set off for Heaven.

The mother was loath to part with her son. "You've come such a long way," she said. "How can you leave like this? If you can't dismount, then at least have a bowl of your favorite pumpkin soup. I remember how you used to love it so. I've just made some, and it should be just about ready now."

The mother went inside the house and soon returned with a steaming bowl of hot soup for her son.

The woodcutter couldn't refuse his mother's kindness and took the soupbowl from her hand, still seated on the horse. But the steaming bowl of soup was so hot that the woodcutter dropped it as soon as it touched his hands.

The soup splashed all over the horse's back. The horse jumped with a start and reared back on its hind legs. The woodcutter was thrown to the ground. With a great neigh of pain, the horse leaped into the sky, leaving the woodcutter behind. In a twinkling of an eye, the horse was gone from sight.

Once again the woodcutter was left on earth. But this time, no matter how he grieved and cried, it was no use. Day after day the woodcutter lifted his face to the sky and called again and again to his wife and his children. But it was too late. Even his friend, the deer, could no longer help him. Day and night the woodcutter yearned to return to Heaven. Day and night he yearned to see his wife and children again. And as he kept gazing up into the sky and calling to his loved ones year after year, he was finally transformed into a rooster.

That is why, when country children today see a rooster crowing on top of a straw-thatched roof, they remember this story told them by their grandparents of the woodcutter crying for his wife and children.

The Magic Gem

ONCE upon a time there was an old fisherman who lived with his wife in a small hut on the bank of a large river. One day, as usual, he went to the river to fish as he was too old to work. All day long he cast his line, but he did not catch a single fish. He thought of returning home empty-handed, but he would not give up and threw his line into the water one last time.

This time there was a big tug and, when he pulled out his line, he found that he had caught a huge carp. The old man was overjoyed. But, as he put the carp into his basket, he noticed that the fish's eyes were full of tears.

On top of that, the carp was opening and shutting its mouth, as if it were trying to say something. The fisherman was suddenly struck with pity for the poor fish.

"Oh, you're trying to say 'Let me go,' aren't you?" he said. "Yes, I understand. I'll let you go."

So, the gentle old man set the fish free in the river. He

then slung his empty wicker basket on his shoulder and set off for
home. He knew that he and his
wife would have nothing to eat
for supper, and would be hungry
again, yet he felt at peace.

The next morning the old man
returned to the river to fish. Suddenly a beautiful young girl stood
before him and bowed politely.
The old man was taken aback and asked: "Who are you?"

The young girl bowed again, and replied: "I am a messenger
from the Palace of the Dragon King. The carp you saved yesterday is really the prince of the Dragon Palace. Thanks to your
mercy, he returned home safely. The King of the Dragon Palace
was deeply moved when he heard how you spared his son's life,
and he wishes to repay you. He invites you to visit him and sent
me to take you back to the palace. Please come with me."

The lovely young girl mumbled some strange words as
though chanting a magic spell. Suddenly the waters of the river
parted in two, and before the fisherman's eyes there appeared a
bright yellow path leading down underneath the water, the likes
of which he had never seen before.

The old fisherman could not tell whether he was dreaming
or not. But he rose to his feet and followed the young girl down
into the river. To his astonishment, he could breathe underwater!

The two walked on and on. Just when it seemed as if the path
had no end, the Dragon Palace suddenly appeared before them.
The sight would have surprised anyone, for it was very grand
and beautiful. The old fisherman had often heard stories of the
Dragon Palace underneath the waters, but never in his wildest
dreams had he imagined he would see it!

The Dragon King was waiting outside the palace and greeted the old fisherman with open arms. The prince also came out
to welcome the old man, and to thank him. "I am the carp you

caught yesterday. I have you to thank for saving my life, yet I do not know how to express my gratitude," the prince said.

The old fisherman felt as if he were in a dream.

They went inside the palace where the king had spread a great feast, and a host of fish began to dance. First a bream, and then a sole, performed special dances for the honored guest.

Many days were spent feasting and merrymaking. But, amidst these pleasures, the old fisherman began to worry about his wife and home. His worries mounted with the passing of each day. He thought how lonely his wife must be all by herself.

The prince noticed how troubled the old man had become and said: "You need not worry any longer. You may return home any time you wish. But there is one thing I would like to tell you before you leave. My father will offer you a gift upon your departure. When he offers you something, you must say you do not want anything but the green gem that is kept in the palace treasure box. As long as you have this magic gem you can wish for anything you desire, and your wish will be granted. Don't forget. Be sure to ask for the green gem."

The old fisherman decided he was ready to return to his wife. As he prepared to leave, the king called to him and said: "I hear you are going home, my good man, and I want to give you a present. What would you like as a remembrance of your stay here?"

The old man recalled what the prince had told him and answered: "The only thing I want is the green gem in your treasure box."

A troubled look came over the king's face. "I cannot give you that," he said, "but I will give you anything else."

The prince then spoke up: "Father, it's true that the green gem is very precious, but remember this man saved my life. I am standing here now—safe and sound—thanks to this old fisherman. The gem is but a small token of his kindness."

"What you have said is true," agreed the king, so he brought out the green gem from his treasure box and handed it to the fisherman. "Take good care of this magic green gem, kind man, and it will take care of you," said the king. The old man thanked the king and prince for their generosity and said goodbye.

The young girl who brought the fisherman to the Dragon Palace led the old man back along the path through the river up to the riverbank, and the fisherman was soon safe in his own home. During the fisherman's absence, his wife had worried constantly. She could not imagine what had happened to him. So she was overjoyed when he returned safely.

The old man told his wife how he had been taken to the Dragon Palace in return for saving the life of a carp, who was really the prince of the palace, and how he had been given a green gem as a farewell present. He brought out the gem and explained that through its power, their every wish would be fulfilled.

The old woman said: "If that's true, let's test it. I wish we had a large and beautiful home." No sooner had she said this than their old straw-thatched hut disappeared, and in its place stood a splendid mansion. The old man and old woman were very pleased.

Next, they wished for rice and wheat and red beans. The magic gem produced as much of these as the old couple desired.

There was now enough food for the two of them to eat for many days.

The green gem brought them whatever they desired—even silver and gold. The old man and woman, who had lived in poverty all of their lives, were now able to enjoy a life of riches.

Across the river lived a mean old woman. When this woman heard of the good fortune that had come to the old fisherman and his wife, she was filled with envy. "I must get that green gem somehow," she mumbled to herself. And she schemed and schemed for a way to get it.

One day, a plan came to her. She waited until the old man was away from home and then dressed herself up like a cloth peddler. Then she called on the fisherman's wife.

"My, what a beautiful home you have!" she said in her most sweet and flattering voice. "I have heard that you were given a magic gem by the King of the Dragon Palace. Please! I'd just love to see what it looks like. Can I see it, just for a minute? I'd like to tell my friends that I've seen the magic gem."

The honest fisherman's wife was completely taken in by the polite manner and flattering tone of the cloth peddler.

"Why, of course," she said. "I'll gladly bring it out to show you."

The goodhearted woman went into her home and brought out the green gem. The false cloth peddler got all excited and ogled the gem. When the kind fisherman's wife saw how anxious the cloth peddler was, she said, "You can hold it if you like," and handed it to the cloth peddler.

"It's so good of you to let me see it," she said. "It is lovely indeed." She turned the gem this way and that and gazed at it from all sides.

Then, while the fisherman's wife was not looking, she slipped the gem into her pocket and took out a green stone that looked like the green gem. But it was only an ordinary stone, without any of the magic powers of the green gem.

"Thank you very much for showing me your treasure," the scheming woman said. "You must take good care of it." Then she handed the false gem to the fisherman's wife and quickly departed.

No sooner had the bad woman gone than the beautiful tiled mansion disappeared and, as the fisherman's wife watched with horror, in place of it there appeared the old straw-thatched hut in which she and her husband had first lived.

"What has happened?" cried the fisherman's wife. "How could this be?"

She suddenly realized that the cloth peddler was nowhere to be found.

"What shall I do?" moaned the fisherman's wife. "How will I explain all this to my husband?" She looked at the miserable shack and cried pitifully, but there was nothing she could do to recover the magic gem.

The fisherman soon returned and was astounded to find that his fine house was gone. "What happened to our home?" he asked his wife.

But the old woman was too grief-stricken to say a word. All she could do was wail and weep. The beautiful mansion, the riches, and the happiness of the old couple were now things of the past. They had faded away like a dream. The old man and woman sat huddled in their miserable hut, not speaking a word to each other, wondering what they should do.

Now, the old man and the old woman had no children, but they did have a pet dog and cat whom they loved dearly. Seeing the old fisherman and his wife wailing over the loss of the green gem and in such a sorry state, the dog said, "Let's get the green gem back for the kind old man and old woman."

"Yes, they have both been good to us all these years. Now is the time for us to try and repay them," the cat chimed in.

The dog and the cat knew that the cloth peddler was really the bad woman from across the river in disguise, so they immediately set out for her house. When they came to the river, the cat got on the dog's back, and the dog jumped into the river and swam to the other shore. They climbed up the bank and saw a large and beautiful house that they had never seen before.

"That must be the house of the bad woman who stole the green gem. The gem must be hidden somewhere inside," the dog said.

The dog and the cat crept up to the house and slipped into the yard to take a good look around. Not knowing she was being spied on, the bad old woman happened to look out from one of the rooms.

"There she is! That's the cloth peddler who came to our home," cried the cat.

Then the cat gently jumped up onto the porch and quickly slipped into the house. There were so many rooms that the cat could not tell where the green gem was hidden. But the clever cat kept peeking into one room after another.

"The green gem is a great treasure. The bad woman wouldn't leave it in just any place. It must be hidden in the innermost room," the cat thought.

So she made her way to the room at the very back of the house. There she spied a cupboard.

"Aha! That would be the most obvious place for her to hide the green gem," the cat thought and quietly opened the cupboard door, just catching a glimpse of the gem. The bad woman must have heard the cat for she came running into the room. "Scat, you cat!" she cried in a huff. "What are you doing here?"

What a frightful face she had! She snatched up the cat and threw her out of the house. Now that the cat knew for sure where the gem was hidden, she went back to where the dog was waiting for her in the yard.

"Did you find it?" the dog asked impatiently.

"Yes, I did," answered the cat, "but the problem now is how to get it back. It's kept in the cupboard in the innermost room."

"Don't worry," the dog replied, "as long as we know where it is, we shall find some way to get it back. But say, aren't you hungry? I'm famished." Neither the dog nor the cat had eaten any supper.

"Let's go and look for some food then," said the cat. So the cat and the dog set off together to find food.

"Where can we find something good to eat?" the cat thought as they prowled through the house. Suddenly, they heard a commotion inside the storeroom. They tiptoed softly to the door and peeked inside. The cat and dog were shocked to find fifty or sixty mice having a grand feast.

They watched the proceedings for a while. Suddenly they

both leaped into the room and the cat pounced on the king of the mice, who was seated in the place of honor. The cat grabbed the mouse by its neck with her paws and pinned it to the floor. The other mice scampered about the room, screeching and squeaking in great confusion.

The cat called out to the mice to be quiet: "Listen, you mice! In the innermost room of this house there is a cupboard. Inside the cupboard there is a green gem hidden away. Bring me that gem immediately. If you do not, I shall eat your king right on the spot!" The cat made fierce eyes and glared at the mice.

The mice were all upset, but they quickly answered: "We shall get the green gem for you. Such a task is no trouble at all. We shall bring it right back to you. Please spare our king."

Then five or six of the mice, the ones with the strongest teeth, scampered out of the storeroom, and sure enough, before long they came back again with the green gem. As soon as the mice handed the gem over to the cat, she thanked the mice and let the mouse king go. Both the cat and the dog were overjoyed that they had recovered the gem.

Just then, they heard the old woman's footsteps. "Now that we have the gem, we have nothing more to do here. Let's get out of here before the old woman finds us! Let's go home as fast as we can and make the old man and woman happy," he said.

Then, completely forgetting their hunger, the two set off for home.

The dog and the cat reached the river. The cat put the precious green gem in her mouth and jumped on the dog's back. The cat slipped a few times, as the dog's fur was wet and slippery, but finally managed to grasp the dog tightly and stay on his back. The dog began swimming across the river. When they came to a point midway between the banks of the river, the dog thought he felt the cat slipping and began worrying about the precious green gem.

"Are you all right? Is the green gem safe?" the dog asked, continuing to swim. The cat, of course, could not answer, no matter how much she wanted to, because she had the gem in her mouth. So she remained silent.

The dog asked again: "Are you sure the gem is safe?" Again the cat was silent.

The dog became very worried and asked the same question four or five times. But each time, the cat gave no reply. Finally, the dog lost his patience and became angry.

"Why don't you answer me?" he shouted rudely. "Can't you hear me? I've asked you over and over again, and you haven't said a single word in reply."

This made the cat angry too. She could keep quiet no longer. She opened her mouth and cried: "Yes! I have it!"

But as she spoke, the green gem fell out of her mouth and dropped into the river. "Plunk!" The precious gem fell right into the water and sank to the bottom.

When the dog heard this noise, he suddenly realized what had happened.

He felt terribly ashamed of his own stupidity. The cat was furious, but the dog felt so bad he couldn't find words to apologize. As soon as they reached the other side of the river, he quietly slunk away home by himself.

The cat could not get over her disappointment. They had gone to so much trouble to get back the green gem, and now it lay at the bottom of the river. The cat sat down by the river, filled with regret and annoyance, and pondered what she should do next. How long she sat there, she did not know. And before she realized it, dawn had already broken, and a fisherman came along in his boat to haul in the nets which he had left out all night. The fisherman began taking fish from the net and throwing them into his boat. It was then that he came upon a dead fish caught in his net.

"This fish is no good. I'll throw it away," he said and threw the dead fish up on the river bank as far as he could. The dead fish landed just beside the cat.

The hungry cat picked it up and was starting to eat it when she noticed a hard bulge in the fish's throat.

She opened the fish up to see what the bulge was. It was the green gem which had fallen into the river!

"The fish must have thought the gem was something to eat," reasoned the cat, "and swallowed it in one gulp. But the gem was so big that it got stuck."

The cat jumped for joy. This time she was not going to lose the gem. She carefully put it in her mouth and hurried home. The old man and the old woman could hardly believe their eyes when they saw their cat carrying the green gem.

Once again, the gem gave them a fine home. It gave them wheat and red beans. It gave them silver and gold. The old man and woman were happy once more.

The old man and woman were so overjoyed that the cat had brought back their precious green gem that they praised her over and over again. Out of gratitude, they allowed the cat to come inside the house and to live there from that time forth, eating the best of foods. In fact, the old couple doted on the cat so much that they forgot all about the dog. So he slept in a corner of the yard and ate nothing but leftover food and fish bones.

Because the cat became the old couple's favorite, and the dog was neglected, the dog became very jealous of her. From that day on the cat and the dog were enemies. And that is why, even today, cats and dogs are always fighting.

The Snake and the Toad

A KIND and considerate young woman once lived in a country villlage. She was very poor and barely managed to eke out a living for herself and her old mother, whom she had to care for all alone.

One day the girl was in the kitchen, just scooping up fresh-ly-cooked rice and putting it into a large bowl to carry to the dinner table. Suddenly a toad appeared in the kitchen as if from nowhere. It crawled over the floor laboriously, dragging its body, right up to where the girl was standing. Then it jumped heavily up onto the kitchen hearth. On the hearth were a few grains of rice which the girl had spilled while emptying the pot. The toad ate up the rice hungrily.

"My, you must really be hungry," the kind-hearted girl said. "Here, I'll give you some more."

And she spilled about half a ladleful of rice out on the hearth. The toad looked up at the girl in gratitude and then gobbled up that rice too, all the while wriggling his puffy throat.

From that day on the girl and the toad became fast friends. The toad did not go anywhere. He made his home in a corner of the kitchen and would come out at mealtimes to eat his share of rice right out of the girl's hands. This way of life continued day after day, until one whole year had passed. By this time the toad had grown into a huge creature.

Now, this village had been troubled for a long, long time by a huge snake that lived in a nest on the outskirts of the hamlet. It was a bad snake. It stole valuable crops from the rice paddies and the vegetable fields. It stole cows and horses. It even kidnapped women and children and dragged them away to its nest, where it ate them up at leisure. This had happened not once or twice, but many, many times.

The villagers knew exactly where the snake's hideout was. Its nest was in a huge cave in a rocky hill just outside the village. Master bowmen and famed marksmen came in turn to the snake's nest to try and kill the monster, but none succeeded. Year after year the snake continued to harass the villagers. The people lived constantly under the threat of death. They never knew when the snake would leave its nest and come snatch them up in its jaws.

The young woman found it hard to sit back and witness this ongoing abuse. She couldn't bear to see the other villagers suffer. She found herself thinking: "The villagers must be saved. There must be some way. Isn't there a good scheme?"

But when bows and arrows and guns had failed to kill the snake, what could one lone girl do? After thinking it over, she finally decided she'd sacrifice her own life in order to save the village from this curse.

"That's it!" she thought. "If a large number of people can be saved, it doesn't matter what happens to me. I'll offer myself up to the snake in exchange for it never terrorizing our village again. Where guns and arrows have failed, my sincere pleas might succeed."

Her old mother was now dead, and she was all alone in the world except for her friend the toad. So, once she had made her mind up, she put on her little shoes with their turned-up toes and slipped out of the house. Just before leaving she called the toad and, wiping the tears from her eyes, said: "We have lived happily together for a long time, haven't we? But today is our last day. I must say goodbye. There will be no one to give you your rice tomorrow. When you become hungry, you will have to go out and find your own food."

The toad, of course, had no way of understanding the language of human beings. But the girl spoke to it in simple and gentle words, just as if she were talking to a child. All the while the toad squatted on the hearth gazing steadily up at the girl's face.

The girl finally wound her way to the snake's nest in the rocky hill outside the village. Forgetting her fear and her sorrow in her desire to save the villagers, she stepped right up to the mouth of the snake's nest. "I have come in place of the villagers to offer you my life," she said. "Please eat me. But, after this, please never again bother the village people."

Nothing happened, so the girl continued to plead her case. Soon night drew near, and darkness began to fall over the countryside.

Finally, when the last light of day faded, the earth began to tremble, and the snake came out of its hole. Its scales were a gleaming green, its red tongue was like a flame. When the girl saw this terrifying creature, she fainted on the spot, falling to the ground.

Just then a single streak of white poison flashed toward the snake. It came from the toad which the girl had cared for with such kindness. No one knew when it had come, but there it was, squatting right beside the girl. And though it was small compared to the snake, it was squirting poison with all its might to protect the unconscious girl.

But the snake wasn't to be beaten so easily. It began spew-

ing poison right back at the toad. Thus the snake and the toad matched poison against poison, the jets criss-crossing in the air like two sharp darts. Neither would give in. This continued for one hour, two hours. There was no sound of clashing swords, no shouts of battle. For all that, it was a deadly fight, waged in grim silence.

Gradually, the snake's poison began to weaken. On the other hand, the toad's poison became stronger and stronger. Still the silent skirmish continued.

Suddenly the snake let out a great gasp and fell down on the rocky hillside. Its body twitched once, twice, and then it finally died. At the same time the toad, worn out with its struggle, fell dead too. The battle was at an end.

A villager passing by the scene of the fighting the next morning found the small girl still unconscious. He took her to her home and nursed her back to health. So not only was she saved, the entire village was too as well—thanks to the heroic struggle of a lone toad the kind young woman had befriended.

Now that the snake was dead, the villagers were able to live in peace and quiet.

The Green Leaf

DAY in, day out, the rain poured down in sheets. The small river flowing by the village rose higher and higher. Eventually the dikes broke, and the muddy water surged through the gap, sweeping everything in its path—houses, people, cows, and horses.

Just then there appeared in the raging waters an old man, rowing a small boat. He was a gentle and kind man. He could not bear to remain in safety while listening to the cries of people stranded in trees and on rooftops. So he rowed his small boat up the river, helping as many people as he could to places of safety.

Just as he was about to leave he saw a small child struggling in the water. He pulled the child into his boat. He next saw a deer swimming by. The deer too he saved. A little while later a snake came swimming by. The old man looked carefully and saw that it had hurt itself. It couldn't swim very well. A snake might not be the best addition to the boat, but the old man felt

sorry for it. He reached into the swirling waters and pulled the snake into the boat.

When he reached high ground, the old man let the snake and the deer go free. But the child had nowhere to go. He had lost his home, his parents, and his brothers and sisters. He was now an orphan. The old man felt pity for the poor little boy. He seemed such a clever fellow, with fine features. Since the old man was childless, he decided to adopt the boy as his own. "From now on you'll be my son," the old man said, and from then on he cared for him as if he were his own child.

The years passed quickly for the happy pair. One day, while the old man was puttering about the house, the deer he had saved during the flood appeared in the yard. It came right up to the old man inside the house and nudged him with his nose as though glad to see him. The deer then took hold of the old man's sleeve in its mouth and started pulling. The deer kept pulling at the old man as though wanting him to follow it.

"You want me to go outside with you, do you?" the old man said. "Yes, that must be it."

So the old man went outside with the deer. The deer kept going on ahead, and the old man followed. As it led the way, the man followed, the deer heading toward the mountains. Up

and up they climbed. The old man didn't know where they were going and had no idea why the deer had summoned him.

Just as they crossed a mountain divide, the deer stopped short and waited for the old man to catch up. There in the mountain was a cave. The deer led the old man to the mouth of the cave and then went in ahead. The old man folllowed. In the middle of the cave he found a large box filled to overflowing with gold and silver, blinding in its dazzling brightness. The old man took this treasure home.

Thanks to the deer, the old man was now very wealthy. He bought a large mansion and many fields and paddies. He came to live a life of plenty. And his son quickly adapted to the good life. He learned to be selfish and extravagant. He spent money like water, he made friends with shady characters and he frittered his days away in idleness.

The old man began to worry over the future of his son. He tried to advise the youngster, but his words fell on deaf cars. Eventually the young man started talking back to his foster father, even spreading an outrageous lie about the man.

"That old man didn't get his money from the deer. That's a lie. He stole all of it during the flood from people who were washed away." This was the lie the youngster spread all over the village.

When the village overlord heard the false accusation, the old man was hauled off to his castle for questioning.

"That's simply not true," the old man insisted. "The deer really did lead me to the money in a cave."

But no matter how earnestly and how often the old man repeated this to the castle officials, they still doubted him.

"Even your adopted son, whom you brought up yourself for so many years, says you stole your wealth," they said. "Isn't that sufficient proof of your crime?" And they threw him into the castle dungeon.

There was nothing the old man could do about it. He spent months in the dank dungeon, waiting to be brought before the judge to hear his sentence.

But one day while the old man sat despondently in the dungeon, something came moving across the floor. It was the snake the old man had saved during the flood. The snake slithered across the cell to where the old man was sitting and suddenly bit him sharply on the shin. Then it quickly slipped out again.

The old man couldn't believe what had happened. "No matter how low I've sunk, to think that it would do such a terrible thing after I went to the trouble of saving its life! I should never have shown pity for that snake." First it was his adopted son and now it was the snake. The old man had saved both from the raging waters, and they had turned against him in ingratitude. The thought of their betrayals made the old man even more despondent. He pressed the painful snakebite with his hands as the tears streamed down his face.

Suddenly the snake slitered back into the cell, this time carrying in its mouth. It was a green leaf. The snake applied the green leaf to the spot where it had bitten the old man and then quickly disappeared again.

Then a strange thing happened. No sooner had the green leaf been placed on the wound than the pain disappeared, and the swelling also went down almost immediately.

"What was the snake trying to do?" the old man wondered. "First it comes and bites me and then it brings a green leaf that heals me. Why?"

A loud commotion outside the cell startled the old prisoner. "It's terrible, terrible!" the jailers were shouting. "What do we do? The lord's consort has just been bitten by a snake. There's no time to call a doctor."

The old man suddenly realized the meaning of the snake's behavior. He shouted: "Let me cure her! I have a natural treatment that's perfect for snakebites!"

The jailers looked doubtfully at the old man. But it was no time to stop and argue. They let the old man out of his cell and rushed him off to where the overlord's wife lay moaning and suffering in pain. All the old man did was to press the green leaf lightly against the snakebite, and she was immediately and completely healed.

The overlord was very pleased and had the old man brought before him. "Where did you get that amazing medicine?" he asked.

So the old man told the overlord the entire story from the time he saved his adopted son, the deer, and the snake in the great flood, until the time the snake appeared in his cell.

"Even a snake knows enough to repay a debt of gratitude. But what a hateful man it is who would betray the foster father who saved his life!" the lord said in great anger. Then the lord ordered his men to bring the young man to the castle and throw him in the dungeon.

The kind and gentle man was loaded with praise and with sumptuous gifts. As a last request, he asked that his ungrateful son be released from prison. The overlord was deeply impressed by the compassion of the old man and immediately granted his request. Then the old man and his son made their way home together.

The youth had learned his lesson well. Not only once, but twice, had his life been saved by his foster father. From then on, he became a changed person and grew into an upright and righteous man. He took good care of his father, and they were able to live a long and happy life together.

The Disowned Student

LONG ago it was the custom for students to head to the quiet and solitude of a mountain temple in order to devote themselves to their studies without distraction. So for three long years, a young man read books and meditated in his mountain retreat. The days passed slowly at first. But one year passed, then two years, and in no time, the three years were at an end. The student had completed his studies and could now go home to his parents.

As he arrived home, who should he find living there but another student, identical to himself in appearance, speech, and manner. He couldn't believe his eyes, a twin, his doppelganger taking his place in the family. But what troubled him most is that his own parents and brothers and sisters wouldn't accept him as a member of the family. They treated him as if he were an imposter. He had come home after all these years, but they would not even let him in the house.

"It's no joke," the young student said. "Can't you see I am your own son? I've just returned from the temple after studying for three years. This one is an imposter," the student pleaded with his family.

The other student burst out of the house, shouting his protests: "Be quiet, you imposter! You're just an old fox trying to fool people. Get out of here before we make you pay for your deception!"

That voice! It was the same as his own. It seemed impossible, yet even his own family couldn't tell the difference between the two. They looked the two youths over carefully. They were wearing the same clothing. They even had the same birthmarks, the same scars. They were exactly alike. The parents then asked them about their birthdays and small details of their childhood and memories of any special occasion that might help solve the problem. But the two youths gave the same answers. As a last resort the parents then asked the two to name each article of furniture in the house, without leaving out an item.

Unfortunately, the real son had been away for three whole years and stumbled in his answers. The other youth, however, had been living in the house for some time and was able to list everything without any trouble.

"Well, that decides it," the family said. "You are the imposter. Be on your way!" So they drove the real son out of the house.

The poor young man was at a loss was at a loss as to what to do. He knew it was useless to argue. He left home, still wondering what he should do. Day after day he continued his exile, wandering lonely here and there.

One day, he met an old priest who gazed kindly into his face and said: "You've had your identity stolen, haven't you? There is someone who looks exactly like you, isn't there?"

"Now here's someone who can help me," the young man thought, surprised at the way the priest had discerned his troubles. So the youth opened up his heart and told the priest how he had returned home after three years of study only to find that another had taken his place in his home. He told also how he had been chased out by his family.

"H'm, h'm," the priest nodded, as he listened to the young student's tale. "Did you ever throw away the trimmings of your fingernails somewhere while you were studying at the temple?"

"Yes," the student answered, "there was a river running right in front of the temple. I used to bathe in that river. Then after bathing, I would sit on the stones nearby and cut my nails. The trimmings I left on the stony river bank."

"Just as I thought," the priest said. "Whoever has eaten your fingernail trimmings has taken over your identity. Go straight home once again. But this time take a cat with you. Hide it in the sleeve of your robe so that nobody knows it's there. When you get home, let the cat out right in front of the imposter. Then the truth will be revealed."

The student did as the priest told him. He hid a cat in his

sleeve and returned home. With everyone gathered before him, he let the cat out of his sleeve, right in front of the person who had taken his place in the family.

As the imposter turned pure white, the cat pounced on him and bit him on the neck. The two struggled back and forth until the imposter fell to the floor, in the middle of the room, his throat cut open by the cat's sharp teeth. The parents and the brothers and sisters looked carefully. There, to their surprise, lay not their son and brother, but a large field rat!

The rat had eaten the clippings of the young student's fingernails and had stolen the youth's identity. The spirit of human beings dwells in their fingertips. When the rat ate the clippings, it was able to assume the form of the young student. But a cat can smell a rat no matter how it's disguised. Thanks to the wise old priest, the student unmasked the imposter and was reunited with his loving family.

The Tigers of Kumgang Mountains

MANY years ago in old Korea, there once lived a very famous marksman and hunter. He was such a fine marksman that he could shoot down a bird in flight, almost without taking aim. Deer and wild boar were no match for this hunter once they entered the sights of his gun. He never missed a shot.

In those days the Kumgang Mountains were full of tigers. The beasts would come down from the mountains and steal, eating whatever they could find, not just horses and cattle, but people too.

There was not a single man who could stop them.

Many hunters set out for the mountains, saying, "I'll get those tigers." But none returned. Instead, they became the prey of the tigers of the Kumgang Mountains.

One day, the famous marksman said: "Now it's my turn. I will kill every tiger in the mountains."

The hunter refused to listen to anyone who tried to hold him back, and he set out to find the tigers.

At the foot of the mountains he came to a lonely inn.

The innkeeper saw the hunter and said: "Alas, are you too going to try to destroy the tigers, only to have them eat you up? Listen to what I say. I'm telling you this for your own good. If you value your life, give up this foolish idea."

The hunter refused to listen. In his heart, he said proudly: "With my skill, there isn't a tiger anywhere that can beat me." Out loud, he said to the woman: "Old woman, just wait and see. I shall come back in a little while, carrying a tiger as big as a mountain on my back." And, laughing to himself, the hunter continued up into the mountains.

That was the last time he was ever seen. Five years passed. Ten years went by. But the hunter did not return.

When the hunter left home, he left behind his newborn son. Now a young man, he had become quite skilled with the gun. In fact, he was almost as good a marksman as his father. The young man knew well why he was fatherless. He had decided long ago that he would shoot and kill the tiger that had eaten his father.

When he reached his fifteenth birthday, the boy went to his mother and said: "I would like to set out for the Kumgang Mountains. Mother, please let me go."

But the mother did not want to lose her son. With tears in her eyes, she tried to stop him: "If even a famous marksman like your father was eaten by the tigers, how can you hope to avenge your father's death? If you go, you will never return. Quit thinking about such things and stay here by your mother's side."

"Don't worry, Mother. I will find the tiger who ate my father and avenge his death." And the son earnestly begged his mother to let him go.

Finally the mother said: "If you want to go so much, you can. But first let me ask you one thing. Your father used to have me stand with a water jug on my head. He would aim at the handle of the water jug from a distance of 1,000 feet, and shoot only the handle without spilling any water. Can you do the same thing?"

When he heard this, the young son immediately tried to match his father's feat. He had his mother stand 1,000 feet away, with a water jug on her head. He took careful aim, but he missed his mark entirely. So he gave up his idea of going to the mountains and practiced three more years with his gun.

After three years, he tried shooting the jug's handle again. This time he succeeded in knocking off the handle without spilling a drop of water.

Then the mother said: "Son, your father was able to shoot the eye out of a needle from 1,000 feet away. Can you do this?"

The son asked his mother to stand with a needle in her outstretched hand. Then he walked back 1,000 feet and, after aiming carefully, took a shot. But he failed to shoot the eye out of the needle. Once again, he gave up the idea of going to the Kumgang Mountains, and settled down to practice even harder.

After three years had passed, he tried the same test again. This time, with a crack of his gun, the eye of the needle fell to the ground.

Of course, his mother had told him a series of lies—hoping that he would give up the idea of going to avenge his father. But now that he was even better than his father, she agreed to let him leave for the Kumgang Mountains. The son was overjoyed and left immediately.

At the foothills he came across the same small inn where his father had stopped years ago. The same old woman was still living there. She asked the young man what he intended to do. He told her how his father had been eaten by the tigers and how he had practiced for years to avenge his death.

The old woman then said: "Yes, I knew your father. He was the greatest marksman in all the land. Can you see that tall tree over in the distance? Why, your father used to turn his back to that tree and then shoot down the highest leaf on the highest branch from over his shoulder. If you can't do the same thing, how can you expect to avenge his death?"

The hunter's son, when he heard this, said he would try. He

placed his gun over his shoulder, took aim, and shot. But he missed. He knew that this wouldn't do, and he asked the old woman to let him stay with her for a while.

From that day on, he practiced shooting over his shoulder, aiming for the highest leaf for hours at a time. Finally, after three years had passed, he was able to shoot down the highest leaf on the highest branch.

The old woman told the hunter's son: "That doesn't mean you can outshoot your father. Why, your father used to set an ant on the side of a cliff and then, from a distance of 1,000 feet, shoot it off without even scratching the surface of the cliff. No matter how fine a marksman you may be, you can't match that!"

Again, the young man then tried to do what the old woman said his father had done. Of course, he failed at first and had to practice three more years before he succeeded.

The old woman had made up stories about his father because she wanted to save the young man. But the hunter's son, without questioning her, had practiced until he could do whatever she said his father had done. The old woman was filled with amazement and admiration.

"You are safe now. With your skill, you will surely avenge your father's death."

The old woman made many balls of cooked rice for him to eat along the way. The hunter's son thanked her and started out along the path leading into the heart of the Kumgang Mountains.

The young man walked deeper and deeper into the mountains. For days and days he wandered through the wilderness. After all, the Kumgang Mountains have twelve thousand peaks and stretch over a vast area, and he had no means of knowing where the tiger lay hidden. In his heart he kept praying that he would be able to find the beast that had eaten his father, and he continued wandering, without any exact destination, through the vast mountain ranges.

One day, while the hunter's son was seated on a big rock taking a rest, a lone priest came up to him and asked: "Excuse me sir. If you have a flint and stone, may I borrow them?"

The hunter's son brought out his flint and stone from the leather purse hanging from his belt and handed them to the priest. The priest struck fire with the flint and stone, and lit his tobacco pipe. As he opened his mouth to take the first puff, the young man caught a glimpse inside the priest's mouth. There he saw sharp fangs such as tigers have.

"Human beings don't have such fangs. He must be a tiger in disguise," the young man thought. Without letting the priest see, he picked up his gun. "But what if he really is a man?" the young man pondered. He hesitated for a moment or two but suddenly felt sure of his suspicion and, raising his gun, let loose a shot at the priest's breast.

With a cry, the priest fell to the ground. The young man looked down; instead of a priest, there lay the dead body of a huge tiger.

After making sure the tiger was dead, the hunter's son continued along the mountain trail. In a little while he came to an old woman digging potatoes in her potato patch. Since the young man was hungry, he asked: "Old woman, would you please give me a potato?"

"I haven't any time to waste," the old woman replied. "My husband was just killed by a bad man. His soul visited me and said that I must hurry and dig up some potatoes and take them to him to eat. Once he eats these potatoes he will live again. That's why I have to hurry."

"That's funny," the young man thought. He looked carefully at the woman's hands. They were not human hands but the hairy paws of a tiger. The hunter's son immediately lifted his gun and took aim. *Bang!* went the gun, and the old woman toppled over and turned into an old she-tiger. The hunter's son continued on his way. In a short while he came upon a young girl carrying a water jug on her head. The young man was thirsty and said: "Kindly give me a drink of water."

The young girl answered: "I'm sorry, but I can't stop. I'm in a terrible hurry. The souls of my father-in-law and mother-in-law came to me and said they have been killed by an evil person. They asked me to bring them water. I must hurry with this water and give it to them so they can live again."

The girl hurried on. From the front she was surely a young girl, but from behind she was a tiger with a long tail. The hunter's son raised his gun and let fly a shot. Down came not a girl, but a young she-tiger.

The hunter's son continued on. Down the road he saw a young man walking hurriedly toward him. The hunter's son called: "Say, won't you sit down with me? Let's exchange talk of our travels."

"No, I can't waste any time. My parents and my wife just came to me in a dream and told me that they have been shot down by a bad man. They asked me to come and offer sacrifices for them. If I delay any longer, it'll be too late for them to live again."

This young man also had a long tail hanging behind him. The hunter's son immediately raised his gun and shot the man dead. By the time the man's body hit the ground it had changed into a splendid young tiger.

The hunter's son was pleased with himself for having gotten rid of four tigers in such a short time. He felt greatly encouraged and continued on his journey, wondering what lay in store for him next.

After a short while he saw a gigantic white animal, as big as a mountain, squatting in the distance. It was a huge, huge grandfather tiger that must have been alive for a thousand years.

The white-haired grandfather tiger opened its great mouth to swallow the hunter. The young man quickly took aim and shot a bullet at the tiger's mouth. But the tiger did not even blink. The young man kept shooting one shot after another at the tiger. But, each time, the grandfather tiger would clench his teeth, draw back his lips, and let the bullets bounce off his fangs harmlessly. Undaunted, the young man kept shooting.

But, in the end, he ran out of bullets, and was swallowed in one gulp, gun and all, by the great grandfather tiger.

The tiger's throat was one black tunnel. Once the hunter had passed through this tunnel, he came to a vast room as large as a fairground. This was the giant tiger's stomach. The hunter was surprised to see the scattered bones of people the tiger had eaten.

He wondered whether he might be able to find the bones of his father and started searching for them. Just as he had thought, he found his father's bones beside a hunting rifle on which his father's name was engraved. The son carefully gathered the bones together and lovingly placed them in the bag hanging on his belt. Then he continued to explore the tiger's stomach.

He came upon an unconscious girl who lay huddled in a heap. The young hunter took the girl into his arms and nursed her back to consciousness.

She looked into his face and thanked him with gratitude. She revealed that she was the daughter of the king's minister, who was famous in the capital. The girl told him how the old grandfather tiger had stolen her away just the night before, while she was drying her hair on the porch of her home.

Though hungry and weary, the two talked over their plight and decided to join forces in finding a way out of the tiger's stomach. They wandered around inside and came to a long empty tunnel. "This must be the tiger's tail," he thought.

The young hunter took a knife from his belt and cut a small peephole near the end of the tiger's tail. Through it they could see outside. They decided that the girl should stay beside the hole and tell the young man whether the tiger was walking through a field, or up some craggy cliff, or along the seashore. The hunter's son then started cutting through the walls of the tiger's stomach. Because the stomach was so thick, he could not make much progress with his small knife. He cut, sawed, scraped, and hacked with all his might. Slowly the hole started to widen.

At first, the tiger was able to bear his stomach pain. But as it increased, he could not keep still.

He went to his doctor friend, an old bear, and said: "My stomach hurts terribly. Have you any good medicine?"

Dr. Bear answered: "That's nothing to worry about. Just eat a lot of fruit and you'll soon be well."

The tiger started eating apples, cherries, pears, and other kinds of fruit—his stomach became like one giant fruit salad! After all, being the huge animal that he was, the grandfather tiger was not content to eat the fruit. He went into orchards and uprooted trees and swallowed them whole! The girl and the young man joyfully plucked the fruit from the trees swallowed by the tiger and filled their own stomachs. Once they had eaten, they felt much stronger and much more courageous. With renewed zeal, the young man worked at cutting through the tiger's stomach.

No matter how much fruit he ate, the tiger's pain grew greater and greater. He went back to see Dr. Bear.

"I don't feel well at all. The pains in my stomach seem to be even worse than before."

"Go to the mineral spring and drink the water there. It's good for stomach aches!" Dr. Bear advised.

The giant grandfather tiger went to the spring and gulped down great volumes of water. The young man and the girl in the tiger's stomach drank the clear sweet water and felt greatly refreshed. The young hunter again renewed his efforts and kept slashing furiously at the tiger's stomach.

Soon the tiger could no longer stand the pain. He ran like a crazed animal. He jumped from high cliffs and ran blindly through forests, knocking himself against rocks and trees. But no matter how he writhed and twisted, he could not stop the pain. Finally, the grandfather tiger ran out of strength and stopped moving.

The girl peeked out from the hole and found that they were in the middle of a large field. She ran to the young man and helped rip open the last remaining bit of flesh separating them from freedom. They then stepped outside safe and sound.

The young man skinned the tiger, for he wanted to take home the beautiful white tiger skin as a present.

Then, taking the girl by the hand, he returned to his home, where his mother was waiting for him. His mother cried tears of joy to see her son come back safely.

After burying his father's bones in the family graveyard, the hunter's son took the girl back to her home in the capital city.

Words cannot describe the joy the king's minister felt when he saw his daughter return home, safe and sound. In gratitude the king's minister celebrated with a grand party and agreed to let the young man marry his daughter.

And they lived together happily ever after in the mansion of the king's minister.

"Books to Span the East and West"

Tuttle Publishing was founded in 1832 in the small New England town of Rutland, Vermont [USA]. Our core values remain as strong today as they were then—to publish best-in-class books which bring people together one page at a time. In 1948, we established a publishing outpost in Japan—and Tuttle is now a leader in publishing English-language books about the arts, languages and cultures of Asia. The world has become a much smaller place today and Asia's economic and cultural influence has grown. Yet the need for meaningful dialogue and information about this diverse region has never been greater. Over the past seven decades, Tuttle has published thousands of books on subjects ranging from martial arts and paper crafts to language learning and literature—and our talented authors, illustrators, designers and photographers have won many prestigious awards. We welcome you to explore the wealth of information available on Asia at www.tuttlepublishing.com.

Published by Tuttle Publishing, an imprint of Periplus Editions (HK) Ltd.

www.tuttlepublishing.com

Copyright text and illustrations © 2024 Periplus Editions (HK) Ltd.

The stories are taken from "The Story Bag" anthology originally appeared in *Negi O Ueta Hito*, published in Japanese in 1953 by Iwanam Shoten, Tokyo.

Library of Congress Cataloging-in-Publication Data in process

ISBN 978-0-8048-5775-8

Distributed by

North America, Latin America & Europe
Tuttle Publishing
364 Innovation Drive
North Clarendon
VT 05759-9436 U.S.A.
Tel: 1 (802) 773-8930
Fax: 1 (802) 773-6993
info@tuttlepublishing.com
www.tuttlepublishing.com

Asia Pacific
Berkeley Books Pte. Ltd.
3 Kallang Sector, #04-01
Singapore 349278
Tel: (65) 67412178
Fax: (65) 67412179
inquiries@periplus.com.sg
www.tuttlepublishing.com

27 26 25 24
10 9 8 7 6 5 4 3 2 1   2405TP
Printed in Singapore

TUTTLE PUBLISHING® is a registered trademark of Tuttle Publishing, a division of Periplus Editions (HK) Ltd.